HORDE OF THE
UNDERWORLD

THE  ASCENSION ARCHIVE

VOLUME ONE

By Dominician Gennari

Dominician Gennari
Melbourne, Australia.

Website:
www.DominicianGennari.com

Social Media:
Facebook: @dominiciangennari
Instagram: @dominiciangennari
YouTube: DominicianGennari

Horde of the Underworld is a work of fiction
created by Dominician Gennari.
Published by **Star Rise Publications** 2022

STAR RISE
PUBLICATIONS

Epub ISBN: 978-0-6454948-3-9
Paperback ISBN: 978-0-6454948-4-6
Hardcover ISBN: 978-0-6454948-5-3

CONTENTS

FOREWORD

In creating the **War for Ascension** saga, I wish to shape a mythical story filled with wonder in a manner to inspire readers to assess the world around them.

These side-quest stories will serve as the glue to coalesce the vast struggles of planet Númaria. Showcasing the richness of my world through a diverse cast of characters, readers will discover aesthetic subtleties in each storyline along with the mirroring adversities we face here on earth.

As the War for Ascension story unfolds, you will appreciate the interplay between earthly axioms and fiction, as they form a cohesive datum to resolve the paradox that we live in a world that is indeed *stranger than fiction*. It is my goal to awaken this curiosity in each reader to explore that which has previously been slandered by our governments and our institutions.

It remains evident to me that many truths can be portrayed in fiction, and adversely, a multitude of propaganda. In a time when our entertainment industry has become more compromised, I stand firm in my resolve to offer you wholesome stories founded in truth, right action, and worthy of your time.

Many of us will look back on these years in consternation, abhorred by the actions of those authors, musicians, and artists who turned their backs on the good people. I hereby stand in my sovereignty as one who enacted truth, and I invite you by my side as we create a new world of art, free from harmful ideologies, and with the power to uplift all to greater heights.

May the candour and veracity scribed upon the pages of my books inspire you.

- **Dominician Gennari,** 2022

PREFACE

The book you're clasping in your hands will serve as the first side story in the **War for Ascension** saga. The events of this chronicle take place nine days after Santia and Areus depart Toria, and it contains all the remarkable elements you'll come to cherish as you delve deeper into my world.

Horde of the Underworld will become one of the multiple volumes in the *Ascension Archive*, and each book will contribute to unveiling the scope of my epic fantasy universe.

Curious about **The War for Ascension** series? Do you want to be part of a new community like no other?

I invite you on this journey of discovery! Join me now at:

WWW.DOMINICIANGENNARI.COM

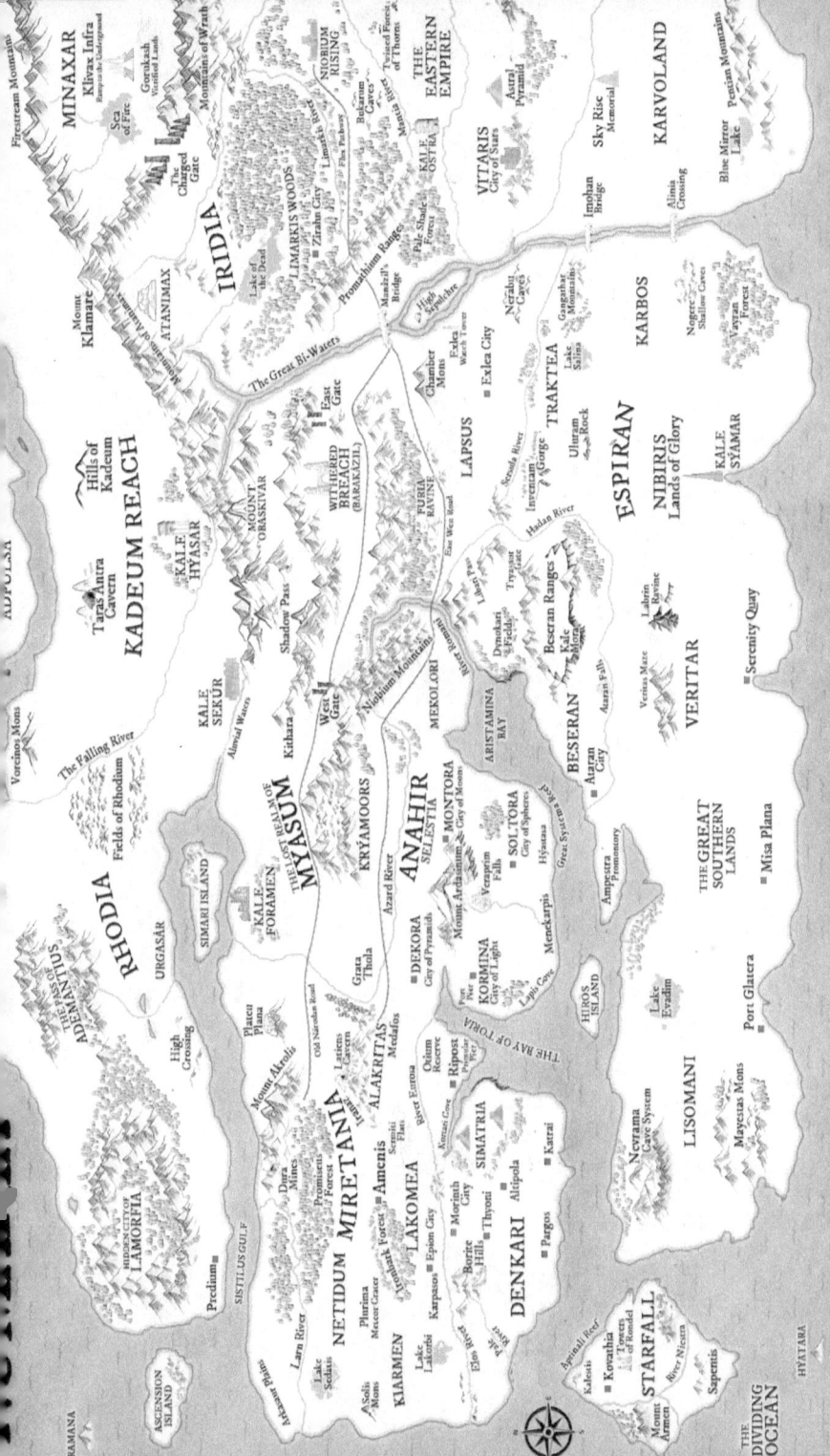

PROLOGUE
A DAY TO REMEMBER

MY NAME IS SYRA, and searching for my eighteen-year-old sister in western Númaria was a task I could never have imagined. The morning sun shines between the grey-trunked larn trees, but my face feels numb from the cold winds streaming through the forest.

It's the tenth day of the eighth month of the year 12,600, and five days ago, the Grandinem Academy declared a student group missing. My sister Telora is one of them. They were last seen near the Miretanian Peninsular of western Netidum.

Being four years older than my sister means I'm the one responsible.

Peering into the misty forest canopy, I rub my gloved hands, but it's not from the cold air drying my skin. It's the fleeting comfort I receive from the action. I gaze into the sloping woodland a bit longer before I march along a suspended walkway, descending a sprawling terrace designed by the ancient race of nomads who once settled in these lands.

I have ten minutes to arrive at a campsite to join a group of fellow mortals in our last attempt to find the missing.

Why we're still searching the southwestern border of the Promiseus Forest during the rise of winter is beyond me. What idiocy would drive Telora down there anyway?

Something doesn't add up.

I want to see my sister again. Help brush her thick blonde hair and listen to her stories, just like we did during the good times. She has no one but me.

The truth is, the real me is a haze of uncertainty. I've learned to swivel through life all these years. I've been hiding, pretending to be someone else. I've failed her as a sister. I'm deceptive. *No. I'm a survivor.* None of it matters now.

Telora, I'll find you even if it kills me.

I step from the walkway onto a winding dirt track and arrive at a two-metre-wide wooden sign.

Gazing upon the signboard, I squint.

Númaria Missing Persons Profile Points

MY STOMACH CHURNS at the thought of not finding her, and I shiver as I stare at the information.

-Point of Separation: Point of disappearance from others.

-Time of Disappearance: Victims go missing mid to late afternoon.

-Boulder Fields: Victims go missing near granite or rock fields.

-Water & Caves: Victims disappear near water sources and cave systems.

-Weather Event: Anomalous weather occurs before or after the disappearance.

-Canine Tracking: Canines are unable to lock onto a scent.

-Missing Clothing: Victims are missing items of clothing or shoes.

The flutter of a Miretanian raven's wings in the nearby trees causes me to flinch. I cover my neck with my scarf and gaze at the scattered granite boulders, which lie before the stone archway entrance to the campsite.

Victims go missing near granite or rock fields. I recall the information.

I close my eyes and wonder what dangers Telora had encountered. It sickens me to think she's alone. Envisioning the better times, I hear her laughter inside my head as if she were standing next to me. I see her smiling at me from the garden of our old home. I can smell her *folina blossom* perfume, and it brings me hope.

In the same breath, it brings me resentment. Anger. Why is this happening to me?

Opening my eyes, I read the profile's final section.

The frequency and rate of missing persons in Grandinem State have increased from ninety-seven to three thousand eight hundred and twenty since last winter. Search and Recover, SAR teams struggle to keep up with the demand.

⚓

TWENTY METRES inside the campsite entrance, I see three tall guards striding toward me. I slow my pace and swallow. What business do the hegemonic Denkarian Soldiers have here? Why are they armed with directed energy weapons and circular shields?

The problem is, I know I'm not supposed to be here without permission from the Denkarians.

"Halt." One of the soldiers extends his arm.

I slow before coming to a pause. I lower my eyes and say nothing.

"I need to see your permit." His brazen voice resonates from the edges of his black helmet.

My hands begin to quiver. *I have no permit. No papers.* I do what I do best. I extend the truth. It's what gets me through awkward situations.

The other two guards flank me, blocking out the sun.

"I'm the SAR coordinator's assistant," I lie to him. "I'm part of the search team, and they're waiting for me, but I didn't know I needed a permit today."

The leading soldier glances grimly at the other two. The corrupt Denkarian senators have mandated identity permits for all who travel within their prefectures. Travelling in convoy regiments, these troopers are dispersed throughout the western lands.

The soldier inches closer. I feel his stale breath ricochet off the skin on my face, and I close my mouth.

"Three thousand Denkari credits," he scolds me, "is your fine without a permit. Or perhaps you prefer to spend the next six months in the dungeons of Alakritas?"

The second soldier aims his weapon at my chest. "The dungeons are perfect for a trespasser like you."

My heart vaults into my throat. "I'm sorry I--"

The soldier cuts me off. "Shut your mouth, you squab-bling brat." He removes his helmet and fires his dark glare at me. "Or I'll break it shut."

His shaven head reveals cranial scars like dry river beds. My breathing becomes shallow, and my palms clammy.

Denkarian soldiers don't like me. It's because of all the

trouble I've given them helping the local resistance known as the Firekites. Some of the Firekites don't even trust me. This is what freedom costs if you can even call it freedom. At least Telora loves me.

A blonde-haired lady calls from up the track. Wrapped inside her long brown coat, she hobbles toward us, waving her hand.

"It's alright," the old lady says, "she's with the search team."

The soldier slides his helmet atop his head and directs his gaze at the bright-faced lady. "Travelling without a permit is a punishable offence, Mirana. You know this."

Mirana stuffs her hand inside her jacket pocket and removes a folded paper. "We have an exemption for non-registered personnel." She hands the note to the soldier. "We need all the help we can get if we intend to find these missing students." She faces me and frowns.

The soldier steps away and whispers to the other troopers. I inhale and hold it. Watching them, I realised how bad this situation could have been. *Thank the heavens you arrived.* I exhale.

"Leave before I change my mind," the soldier barks, shoving the unfolded paper in Mirana's face.

Mirana takes the paper and places it inside her pocket. Clasping my arm, she marches me to the campsite.

I wait until we pass them before talking. "Thank you."

"You should have your permit," Mirana says. "The Denkarians control things here and everywhere else."

"I'm not registered in their 'citizen monitor' system," I confess to her. "I don't think it's fair the Denkarians surveil and dominate every part of our lives."

Mirana doesn't speak a word. She doesn't need to because her sullen eyes and silence convey more than words. The few sane mortals of the west are fed up with the effective slavery system of the corrupt elite. Why are people still complicit with the ruling Denkarian families? Why do we continue to follow the orders of these sociopaths? They hate our existence. To them, we are the scourge upon the lands. The elites don't necessarily want us all dead because who else would do their dirty work? Who else will serve them like the compliant and suggestible slaves we have become?

Wind rustles the trees, and I breathe in the chilling air as I take deep strides. The crunching leaves beneath my feet amplify, and I glance at the gathering volunteers beyond the gate ahead.

Will the people of Netidum stand up to these pernicious men and women of the elite cabal families? Will someone come to save us? What will it take before our populace awakens? How much punishment awaits our people, or have we descended so far into apathy that there will be no attempt to reclaim our sovereignty?

My heart throbs at the thought of never seeing my sister again. *How did it come to this?* I struggle to understand my dilemma.

I have a feeling this day may not end well.

CHAPTER 1
AN INVITE TO DANGER

THE HIGH-PITCHED VOICE of SAR coordinator Marius echoed above the campsite of the southern Promiseus Forest. The camp was a six hundred square metre clearing girdled by the golden-leafed mixtura trees endemic to the western region. On the west side, two large, white tents were filled with people registering for their search sectors.

Smoke wafted from a large fire pit near the campsite's centre, where tables of bread and fried eggs were being served to the volunteers.

Marius addressed the group of two hundred mortals atop a one-metre-high flat boulder. Desperate to find her sister, Syra clasped her pack, zipped up her blue jacket, and weaved to the front of the group. She pulled the fringe of her curly brown hair behind her ear.

The smell of diamond leaf tea wafting from flasks throughout the campsite made her sick. She hated diamond leaf tea and all its stimulating effects. *Why would anyone drink that bitter, spicy tea?* She scoffed and fanned the steamy tea away from her face.

The distant barking of the confused, short-haired

hounds lifted into the forest canopy. She noticed the SAR ground teams had set up bump lines and search grids with strings crisscrossing the eastern woodlands to her left. *So much string it looks like a giant spider's web.*

"Gather round," Marius called. He buttoned his orange SAR jacket up to his neck and ran his finger along his paper map. His receding grey hair was whisked in the breeze. "We've been hard at work searching for any clue of the missing group.

"As you know, we've fallen short in our findings. We're yet to locate the exact point of their access into the forest, and there's still no sign of their transporter. That's why our search will favour the eastern border today."

A shiver darted from Syra's shoulders to her neck as a flood of reactive thoughts was triggered. *How can I survive this cold? I can't even light a fire. I haven't eaten properly in days. I could be stuck somewhere or injured? I could be--*

A voice emanated from behind her, severing her thought stream.

"I'm Tion," he said, "an environmental specialist from Southern Grandinem. May I make a suggestion?"

Syra turned to see the fit-looking middle-aged man with dark blond hair. He stepped forward, fastened his brown scarf about his neck, and retrieved a folded map from his pocket. A tall woman with lissom features stood beside him, pulling her long blonde hair through the shoulder strap of her backpack.

Tion unfolded his map. "My wife, Kardia, and I wish to take a specialised group to the northern borders of the forest." He stared at his wife.

"I study the local wildlife," Kardia said. "I work for the Grandinem Wildlife Sanctuary."

"What area of the northern borders exactly?" Marius enquired.

"Mount Akrolis." Tion lifted his map and pointed to the mountain range. "It's an area we haven't searched."

Syra heard the ambience of dissonant voices and whispers in the crowd. The surrounding bodies shielded her from the crisp winds as vapours issued from her mouth. She thought about Tion's daring proposal and felt hope swelling inside her heart. *If there's a chance at finding Telora, this is it.*

Marius buried his face in his map. "It's a long way, but you're right. It's an area we haven't searched." He raised his head. "Who will accompany Tion and Kardia?"

Just as Syra was about to raise her hand, a voice bellowed from the middle of the group.

"We'll accompany you," a young man shouted. He stood, gleeful, beside another younger, slightly taller man.

Syra gazed at the two lean spry men, dressed in green scouting uniforms with bright yellow stripes and wearing oversized hiking boots. Pliers, compasses, flasks, and ropes dangled from their pockets and jackets as they bumped their way to the front of the group.

"I'm Blaze," the young man shouted. "This is my brother, Turtle. We're the sons of the renowned mountaineer, *Hike*. We know Mount Akrolis well."

Syra heard the rising murmurs among the crowd. She saw heads nodding as they muttered in recognition of the renowned mountaineer and local hero, Hike.

Marius glanced at Blaze and Turtle. "We have an environmental specialist, a wildlife steward, and two mountaineers. Do we have any willing healers or first responders?" He darted his gaze around the group of volunteers.

A short man wearing a green coat stepped forward. "I can help, but I'm no healer."

Marius shook his head. "Sorry, I'd prefer a healer or first responder to accompany them."

No one, not even the SAR coordinators, had suggested such a path. Far from being a healer, Syra did not even know where her kidneys were situated inside her own body. Working a pointless job at the local store never allowed for such expertise. The worst she had seen was a young shop hand slice into his thumb. She had passed out from the sight of his blood.

Her face went red. Her palms became sweaty. Not at the thought of lying. To her, lying was a coping mechanism. She was becoming more aware of her lies. *They'll never guess I'm not a healer.* Her gut sank, and her heartbeat pulsated up into her neck.

Mustering her bravado, she pushed forward. "I'll join them." She raised her hand, ambling through the crowd. "My name is Syra, and I'm a healer from Epion City, Lakomea." She lowered her eyes in shame at her lie.

Marius paused and squinted, staring straight at her. A hush of voices rose within the group. Her transforming anxiety overthrew her analytical mind. *Can I fool him?*

Marius gave her a taut smile. "Alright, Syra," he said.

His acknowledgement of her was a slight reprieve for such a superficial lie.

Marius descended the large rock and gathered Tion, Kardia, Blaze, Turtle, and Syra.

"Turtle?" Syra questioned the young man. "That's your real name?"

Turtle ran his fingers through his hair, exposing his freckled cheeks. "Yeah, it's Turtle."

"You want us to call you Turtle?" Syra's forehead was creased.

"Ah . . . yes, that's my name."

Syra chuckled. "You can't be serious about it."

"Do I look serious now?" Turtle poked his tongue out at her.

Syra gasped at the length and curvature of his tongue, and though she knew his action was playful, it seemed inappropriate.

"Enough, you two." Marius quieted them with his quick voice. He waved his hand in front of the other volunteers. "Attention, everybody. The rest of us will begin our search due east in exactly ten minutes. Meet back here for your allocated search sectors."

The volunteers, mainly middle-aged women and men, dispersed into smaller groups. Syra heard voices calling here and there. Smaller campfires were snuffed, and people foraged through bags and storage containers. Tents were packed, and shoes and straps were adjusted for the long day ahead.

Marius drew closer to Tion. "What route do you plan to take?" His voice sounded hesitant.

"North Forest Road, to Larn River," Tion answered. "The west bank of the river is known among locals to be a treasured fossil site."

"They weren't meant to travel that far north," Marius told him.

Tion nodded. "I understand, but they may have decided to explore the area. I'm familiar with a trail leading up to the pass of Mount Akrolis. It'll take two hours to get there. We'll need to travel on foot through the mountain pass."

Turtle stepped forward. "That's where we'll come in

handy." He stood with his arms folded and his feet shoulder-width apart.

Blaze smirked and assumed his brother's stance with his arms folded. "We know of a track that'll bring us to the Larn River in a fraction of the time."

Syra stared at the brothers with caution. *They're so sure of themselves.*

"A shortcut?" Tion questioned Blaze.

Kardia glanced at Blaze. "You're not thinking about descending the Akrolis Ranges?"

Blaze smiled at his brother. "That's not what we had in mind. There's a path, or, should we say, an access tunnel leading underground."

Syra imagined the cold, dark underworld and all the aversions it had to offer. "You want to take us underground?" her voice was taught, and her face tensed.

"It'll save us hours." Blaze unlatched the lid of his steel flask and sipped a mouthful of water. "Leaving more time to search the river area."

"Do you mean the old mining tunnels?" Tion asked.

"Yeah, through the Dura Mines," Blaze said. "Our father used to take us there when we were younger." He nudged Turtle, knocking him off balance.

"Your father might be well known," Syra said, "but going underground sounds dangerous." She gawked at Blaze with her hands on her hips. "And your arrogance annoys me. No offence to you."

"You've mistaken my confidence for arrogance." Blaze gave her a big smile. "You'll thank me when this is done."

Marius squinted his beaming eyes at the brothers. "Those old mining tunnels were decommissioned millennia ago. I don't advise you to go that way."

Tion glanced at Kardia before facing Blaze. "How treacherous are those caverns to move through?"

"We were in there the summer before last," Blaze said. "A few tight squeezes here and there. It's a little damp in some places. Apart from that, we'd be out in thirty minutes."

Syra pointed at him. "I thought we were searching Mount Akrolis, not some cave system."

The thought of being trapped in the dark underground made her shiver, but the idea of not seeing her sister strangled her heart.

"Tion, Kardia, Syra," Marius said, "it's your decision to take this proposed route."

Tion clasped Turtle's arm. "You say we'll be underground only for thirty minutes?"

Turtle gazed about the group. "We'll have you all out in thirty minutes, I swear."

"Alright, then," Marius said, "can we agree on this route or not?"

Syra paused. She could feel their gazes on her. She felt as if Marius was really asking for her validation. *Going off course to visit some fossil site during winter? How reckless.*

The shoulder straps of her pack dug into her.

Staring at the trees bending in the wind, Syra remembered the summer days spent with Telora at the family ranch. Chasing her in the garden. Eating the ripe amyntus berries until her stomach bloated.

Syra's life up to this moment seemed too much like a pathless wood, where unruly branches scratched her and cobwebs tickled her into discomfort. *I was once a good sister.* She continued to envision the better days. Her tired vision transferred back to the group.

"We'll take the underground route." Syra pulled her

beanie over her head. "We might have a chance of finding them, right?"

Kardia and Tion nodded at her.

"I want all of you back before nightfall," Marius ordered them with a commanding voice. "I'm placing Tion in charge. Blaze and Turtle will lead you through the mines. Don't hesitate to turn back. Is this clear to everyone?"

Syra quivered at the idea of entering the ancient tunnels of the Dura Mines. Fables of the underworld had been told to them as kids to make them fear the darkness below, but they were just stories. *I'm cold. I'm conflicted. I'm frightened, but I need to find Telora.*

Syra stared at Tion and Kardia as they packed their flasks, lamps, and food stores into their backpacks. Blaze and Turtle could not fit anything else into their packs or on their bodies.

Tion latched his backpack. "Be sure you bring enough food and water for the journey to Mount Akrolis." His eyes scanned the group.

Syra searched her pack for her binoculars, but instead, she grasped the handle of her hunting knife. Unsheathing the seven-inch steel sharpened blade, she examined its sabre grind stonewash finish. The black wooden handle had the initials S.D. etched in bronze, the last remnant of her deceased father.

Syra believed the blade was imbued with magical powers. Her father had given her the knife. It had saved his life six years ago during a thylacine attack in Alakritas. She imagined the raging maw of the four-legged, monstrous thylacine. Snarling. Howling. She squeezed the blade's handle.

One day it might save my life.

CHAPTER 2
POINT OF SEPARATION

"WHERE'S YOUR HEALING SATCHEL?" Kardia asked Syra.

Syra froze, unable to find a suitable answer. *What on Númaria is a healing satchel?* She kept her head down and continued to forage through her backpack. Breathing heavily, she felt her lie beginning to crumble. *What have I gotten myself into? I should've seen this coming.*

Turning her head to the right, she saw a black pack with a small healer's symbol, two white circles separated by a white vertical line, sitting at the base of a larn tree. Syra was no healer but was witty enough to notice the word 'Heal' below the symbol on the bag.

"My satchel is over there," Syra said, pointing at the tree. "Turtle, can you get it for me?" She lowered her head, pretending to look busy.

Turtle gave her a half-satisfied smirk before racing over to collect the satchel. He dumped it at her side.

Kardia unlatched the bag, and Syra watched her sort through all the little packages and compartments. "Looks like you've got everything you'll need," she said.

Syra tensed and nodded as she lowered her gaze.

"A folding splint." Kardia unbuttoned a secondary compartment inside the satchel. "Trauma dressings, gauze, bandages. You've got a small vial of baylis liquor for cleaning wounds, burn dressings and ironbark tree oil."

"You can never be too prepared," Syra mentioned as she closed the satchel lid. "I think your husband is ready to go." She pointed to the southern region of the campsite.

Tion hopped into the driver's seat of his matte-grey transporter and powered up the hull. The transporter hummed as it levitated above the ground.

Kardia yanked the side door open, and the rest took their places inside. Kardia leaped inside and closed the door.

Tion steered slowly out of the campsite, steering north along a three-metre-wide track leading to the outskirts of the Promiseus Forest.

The rays of the mid-morning sun streamed through the transporter's windows. Syra smelled the scent of damp pine bark pouring through the air vents. Slopes trailed one hundred metres from the side of the track, sinking into bush-covered trenches. To the northeast, she saw the peaks of Mount Akrolis rising, argent and immense.

She closed her eyes and daydreamed for what seemed like a moment, but almost two hours elapsed in her lacking consciousness.

She felt the tug of the transporter ease. She opened her eyes, and to her surprise, they had finally reached the base of Mount Akrolis.

"The mountain's elevation exceeds twelve hundred metres," Tion said, steering into a small grassland clearing. "Though we won't be ascending to such heights, you may experience some high-altitude symptoms."

Syra's gaze climbed to the peaks of the mountain. "Why are you slowing?"

"Look." Kardia pointed. "Between the slopes."

Lowering her stare, Syra spotted a green and brown object tucked away behind many bushes and scattered branches. At first glance, she noticed the thing was large and curved at its top edges. As they drew near, she saw a horizontal, orange stripe along what appeared to be an abandoned hull.

Kardia unlatched her seat belt. "Seems like we're in the right place."

Blaze flicked Turtle's arm. "I knew they'd come this way. What did I tell you?"

Tion brought the transporter to a halt.

Syra opened the door first, and they marched to the hull projecting from the bushes. She saw the Grandinem Academy badge shining through the covering of larn branches. *Why is it covered in vegetation?*

The green and brown transporter blended into the terrain well. She watched Tion and Kardia peer through the window of the abandoned transporter. She pressed her nose against the cold window, shielding her eyes from the sun. *No sign of damage or breakdown.*

Tion knelt and ducked his head underneath the hull. "The lower strip is intact. No damage to the outside." He stood up and slid the door open. He flicked the power button. "No power. That's probably why they couldn't locate the transporter's beacon."

"No mains power?" Kardia questioned. "I thought a transporter's beacon didn't rely on it."

Tion shrugged. "Maybe it's a magnetic fault?"

Syra popped her head inside the hull. "Why would they leave their tents and camping gear behind?"

"Makes no sense to me," Tion said.

Blaze and Turtle waited outside.

Kardia pointed to the piled provisions and equipment at the back of the transporter. "Flasks, bread, and backpacks just left here."

"You think they'll be far, Tion?" Syra asked.

Tion twisted and glanced at the mountain. "The most likely place is the fossil site at Larn River."

"Should we take the mountain pass?" Kardia asked Tion. "In case they took that known route?"

"That trail could take hours," Tion remarked. "A day even. The underground path will be quicker."

Kardia lowered her voice. "Something doesn't feel right about going underground."

A transcending force drew Syra's mind to the underground path ahead.

She imagined a deep blackness. Not the simple emptiness of a dark hall, but more like a cold and foreboding netherworld beneath the lands she knew, filled with spiders, trolls, and worse.

She swallowed, and the anxiety building inside her flooded her airways, leaving a dry pain in her chest. She began panting, struggling to inhale deeper breaths. She clasped her chest and felt the weight of her head and shoulders hunching. She stumbled and clung to the door handle of the transporter.

Kardia clasped her hand. "Are you alright, Syra?"

Syra gasped, and her eyes widened. She lifted her gaze to Kardia, feeling her warm touch. "I've never been underground," Syra confessed.

Beyond the fear of treading underground and as stupendous as it sounded to her, the mines offered what no one else could, an opportunity of seeing Telora again.

Tion leaned to Kardia. "Let's just get it over and done with." He kissed her forehead before facing Syra. "We shouldn't delay." He leaped out of the transporter and marched to a narrow dirt track winding northeast. The company followed him to Mount Akrolis.

The track on the side of the mountain remained easily traversable as they strode for six kilometres. Syra wiped her damp brow with her sleeve in the intense winter sun. She felt tiny droplets of sweat trickle along her spine. She began to breathe heavily. She was lean, but she was unfit.

On the east side of the track, she noticed many cone-shaped mud structures over two metres high, made by red, swarming insects half the size of a thumbnail. A squawk resonated above, and she saw a phalanx of Miretanian pterosaurs gliding through the western skies.

"Take a break here." Tion slowed his pace to a halt.

Syra's shoulders hurt beneath the weight of her pack. She sighed and slung her backpack on the short grass to the side of the track. Blaze and Turtle sat on the grass and mumbled to each other.

"Is anyone else exhausted?" Syra flipped the lid of her canister and guzzled a throat full of water.

"How long have you been a healer?" Kardia asked.

Syra coughed and choked on her water at the question. She wiped her wet mouth, unsure how to reply. She said the first thing on her mind. "Ahh, four years."

Kardia raised her eyebrows. "You seem young for a healer of four years. How old are you?"

"I'm twenty-seven next month," Syra lied.

"Which Healing Academy do you belong to?" Kardia enquired.

Syra kept her mouth shut. The further she maintained

her lie, the faster she descended. She justified her lie by reminding herself of her purpose. *Find Telora.*

"Blaze," Tion called to him. "Mark the path leading to the tunnel entry on my map." He handed a pencil to Blaze and picked up his pack. "Let's keep moving." He hurried along the track, striding west of the mountain.

Without answering Kardia's question, Syra leaped to her feet and followed Tion. The track narrowed as the slopes of the mountain converged, shading the group from the sun. Grey clouds began to form like patches of conjoined cotton.

The path inclined at a twenty-degree angle and fell at a forty-degree angle. Syra felt her calf muscles tightening with each step she made.

After six hundred metres of descent, the group entered a clearing of flat grassland.

A further three hundred metres ahead, Syra began to feel the ground harden beneath her heels. She gazed upon the nearby terrain and saw a paved path of smooth bluestone emerge from the grass beneath her feet.

"The surface has changed." Syra pointed at the ground.

"The ancient entrance path." Tion leaped into a jog.

Blaze, Turtle, and Kardia sped after him.

Syra turned east and saw a tall, grey megalithic pillar rising from the ground. Its edges glinted in the stream of sunlight, which pierced through the fluffy clouds. The sight of the monolith sent a chill along her spine.

She glanced at the bluestone path beneath her feet. She panned her gaze about the lands and felt a looming presence as if she was being watched from afar by some unseen force.

CHAPTER 3
PATH TO THE UNDERWORLD

DRAWING NEAR THE THREE-METRE-HIGH MONOLITH, Syra stared at the smooth, dark andesite pillar. To her surprise, the stone was still sharp at its edges.

"It's incredibly preserved." Kardia rubbed her fingers across the megalith's surface. "Even after thousands of years."

Syra ran her index finger upon the carved characters and symbols adorning the stela. "I can't read the symbols, but they're graceful. Perfect."

"Don't worry, we can't read them either," Turtle said. "Our father told us what some of these symbols mean." He pointed to four bold words at the top of the stela. "*Dura Minaxon, Aditus Proti*, which means Fortified Mines, First Access Point."

"There are four access points in total," Blaze told them. "Turtle, what are they called again? You know, the other symbols?"

"Ahh . . . *Aditus Proti, Aditus Detar-De-tori* something, some--"

Blaze cut his brother's speech. "*Aditus Proti, Aditus Déteri, Aditus Tréti,* and *Aditus Tédhara.*"

Tion glanced at Kardia. "Ancient Kynorian numbers, one through to four." He strolled along the path. "The old master at the last academy I worked at was obsessed with the Kynorians."

Kardia, Blaze, and Turtle followed him.

Syra took one last glimpse at the monolith. With mouth agape, she stared at the symbols. She had heard rumours about the Kynorians. High Kings. Proud Queens. Powerful Mages. Some even said they were gods. Those were the rumours. *Their civilisation must've been incredible.*

"Syra," Kardia called. "You coming?"

She peeled herself away from the monolith and leaped up the path.

After five hundred metres, Syra could see pentagonal andesitic pillars flanking the path leading up to the entrance of the mines. Ancient Národan runes were carved vertically onto each two-metre-high pillar. The runes were angular, with vertical and horizontal lines connecting each character.

Syra fixed her vision to the north, and less than one hundred metres ahead, she saw a grand opening carved into the mountainside. She had seen nothing of the like, fashioned by the skilled hands of the ancient races.

Drawing near, she saw the arch of the ten-metre-high entrance was recessed with parallel steps. Národan runes were inscribed upon the keystone of the arch. Kynorian letters were etched upon each side of the entrance.

Near the left entrance pillar stood a metallic plaque with an engraved map. The map drew Syra's attention.

She stared upon the detailed three-point perspective image of the mines and each point of access. The bottom left of the map displayed an index of entrances, bridges, and connecting passages.

Blaze pointed at the plaque. "Father said these plaques fronted each of the four entrances, set up for the Kynorian and Národan miners to navigate the tunnels. Some say these plaques were made of metal, not from our planet."

"How would your father know that?" Syra smirked at him.

"He knew many things." Turtle fired his words at her.

"The brothers are right," Tion defended them. "The ancient Kynorians and Národan delved for precious metals and gems, which they crafted into works of insurmountable beauty and technology."

Most of this knowledge was beyond Syra or any of them. The Denkarian elites deemed all knowledge of the previous civilisation conspiratorial. Any discussion about the ancient Kynorians was carefully curated out of the society's awareness by the appointed chancellors of their learning institutions.

Those individuals who dared to challenge the Denkarian institutions were destroyed either physically or shunned publicly.

For a moment, Syra forgot she was entering the underground, distracted by the heritage before her eyes. *How does a civilisation this advanced simply disappear?*

"They had powerful technology hidden underground," Turtle added.

Blaze nodded in agreement. "It's magical technology they could control with their minds."

Syra scrunched her face. "That's impossible. You're lying."

"No, I'm not." Turtle shook his head forcefully.

"He's not lying!" Blaze exclaimed.

"If it's true," Syra said, "why haven't we seen anything like it?"

Blaze's eyes bulged. "Because their technology was inter-dimensional."

"What do you mean by 'interdimensional'?" Kardia asked him.

"Their technology," Blaze said, glancing at Turtle. "It couldn't be seen by our mortal eyes. It exists in a different dimension, a dimension we can't see or understand, and that's why they could control it with their minds."

Syra folded her arms. "I still don't believe you."

A moderate wind blew across the entrance, spraying dead leaves and dust about them. The company gathered closer, shielding their faces from the winds.

"Enough interdimensional talk." Tion's voice was firm. "Blaze, Turtle, you can take it from here. We stay together down there. We remain within eyesight of each other. The underground is dark, in case you didn't know. I suggest you have your lamps ready. Under no circumstances do we sepa-rate." He gazed upon them with a grim face.

Syra stared past the threshold and shivered.

The brothers had already retrieved their lamps from their packs.

"We'll go at a steady pace," Blaze assured them. "Call if we're moving too fast." He marched through the entrance with Turtle behind him.

Tion nodded at Kardia, and with a deep breath, he entered. Kardia followed him.

Syra twisted to glimpse the warm sun illuminating the lands. The afternoon breeze brushed against her face. Her movements were clumsy as she tried to find her lamp inside her pack. She had done this so many times, gotten herself into unforeseen situations, but nothing like this.

"Syra." Kardia's voice echoed from inside the tunnel.

"Yeah, I just had to get my lamp ready." Syra closed her eyes and inhaled. *What am I doing, going underground?* She exhaled and opened her eyes. She switched her lamp on and stepped across the threshold into the cold, binding darkness of the Dura Mines.

Their footsteps echoed and fell upon the dense stone walls. Blaze strolled ahead of them, descending the steps. His lamp lit the path before him. The winding stone steps were perfectly flat and undamaged as if they had been made mere moments before they entered.

Syra inhaled and exhaled controlled breaths, and she distracted her anxious mind by counting each step. *Four hundred fifteen steps.*

After five minutes, they arrived at a foyer with dusty polished-concrete floors. Syra aimed her light at the rising black-glass walls adjoined to flying buttresses that framed a geometrically-patterned, vaulted ceiling above. Leaf-like shapes mantled the niches in the walls, and vertical glyphs with slanted lines and small circles were scribed every five metres.

The air inside the foyer was crisp, and the condensation trickled down the glass. The lights of the company flicked from wall to wall. They strolled to the end of the foyer and descended a wide stone ramp. Syra could smell the dampness as the path wound to the right and left a few times before steadily levelling.

"What an array of biodiversity." Kardia shone her light at the one-metre-wide garden beds on the left side of the wall.

Mosses, lichens, and fungi sprawled across the bluestones, climbing up the walls where water had seeped. Bright yellow, six-legged insects with bulbous bodies crept along the channels and crevices to the side of the path.

Blaze and Turtle strode ahead, increasing the group's pace. The ceiling lowered, and the path narrowed as it merged into a semi-circular tunnel with mottled, dark walls as if they had been cauterised long ago. The tunnel dipped and wound until the walls widened and the ceiling elevated.

"Kardia, over here," Tion called to her, directing his light to the old carting wagons on the right side of the tunnel. "This equipment has been stagnant for years but look at the shine on that wheel." He buffed the metallic rim using his shirt to reveal a brilliant chromium surface.

"*Aditus Proti,*" Blaze said, "was one of the main areas the Kynorians quarried."

Syra aimed her light at the steel cart. "We learned nothing about the ancient days at school."

"Thank the devious Director General for that," Tion said. "Anything to do with the ancient Kynorians is deemed not only non-essential but conspiratorial. They really don't want us to know the past."

"Little is known of the Kynorians." Kardia aimed her lamp at the cobweb-covered lighting system lining the upper walls. "At least outside of their land called Starfall. Even less is known about this place."

"Let's keep moving." Blaze shook his lamp in his hand and trudged upon the path.

They followed Blaze's pacing strides for two hundred metres as the path rose and fell. In the distance, Syra could see granite benchtops, alloy buckets, and stone shelves with compartments the size of a washing basket.

A mound of purple crystals on a nearby benchtop glinted in Syra's light. "What were these benches used for?"

Kardia placed her hand on Syra's shoulder. "Probably used for inspecting the precious ores."

"Look here." Tion pointed to the opposite side of the chamber.

Next to the ledges stood a two-metre-high megalith with the elegant etchings of the *Ipsil Keri*, the ancient script of the Kynorians. Opposite the megalith stood two seven-foot-tall statues of a high Kynorian king and queen. The sight of the statues took Syra's breath away.

Slender crowns fashioned from some type of translucent glass-like alloy mantled the heads of the king and queen. A bright green jewel sat at the centre of the queen's crown, and a shining citrine jewel was on the king's crown. The precision of the sculpting was beyond anything Syra had ever seen. The marble statues at Grandinem Towers on Sunrise Promenade seemed like the hand's work of a novice compared to the creations of the Kynorians.

"I've never met a Kynorian," Syra said. "Have you, Kardia?"

Kardia shook her head. "These statues are so realistic I feel like having a conversation with them." She smiled.

Syra could not take her eyes off the statues. *Her almond-shaped eyes. Her facial symmetry. His chiselled face and V-shaped torso.* Entranced by their elegance, Syra questioned herself. *Maybe the brothers are right. Perhaps the Kynorians were magical?*

Tion shone his light on another ledge, revealing transparent tools. "I read in a forbidden archaeology journal a few years back that the Kynorians and the Národan were specialists in metallurgy."

Upon the granite bench lay a semi-circular knife, a diamond-tipped power saw, and what seemed to be a transparent axe. The double-edged axe had a thick grip, and the haft slightly curved beneath its shoulder. The blade appeared broader and longer on one side.

27

Kardia removed the axe from the ledge and handed it to Tion. "This must be some sort of metallurgical foundry then."

"That's strange." Tion squinted at the axe. "Here. Feel it." He handed the axe to Syra.

"It's cold and hard like steel," she said in surprise at the weapon. "Bizarre. It's see-through like glass. I'm no scientist, but how's that even possible?"

Tion shrugged.

"I told you, they've got magical technology." Turtle flashed his lamp in Syra's eyes.

"Stop it, you imbecile." Syra slapped his lamp away.

"Hey, can anyone smell that?" Turtle pinched his nose.

A fetid smell blew in from the thin slits upon the upper walls of the chamber.

"Smells like a mixture of soil and sulphur." Kardia covered her mouth.

"It smells like acidic faecal matter." Syra's olfactory system was flooded with the stench.

"It'll taper off the farther we go," Blaze assured them. "We're getting close to the damp, tight section of the journey I talked about."

CHAPTER 4
THRESHOLD OF NO RETURN

"HOW FAR IN ARE WE, BLAZE?" Tion enquired as he switched his light from wall to wall.

Syra felt her stomach squelch from the lack of food. The truth was, she never had food in her pack, and she was too proud to ask the others for any. She never thought she would be gone long enough to need it, and with the little money she had, Syra only ate once a day. She flipped the lid of her flask and glugged a long drink.

"Just over a quarter of the way," Blaze answered confidently, aiming his light at a corridor leading away from the foundry chamber. "The path will drop steeply, so cut an angle as you walk down like I do."

Syra waited for them to pass her, quietly sliding the Kynorian axe into her pack. *It could be worth something.* They marched farther along the corridor until Blaze halted before the declining path.

Following his advice, they side-stepped all the way to the bottom landing.

"See, nothing to worry about," he said from the landing below.

"Easy for you to tell us." Syra stretched her thighs. "All this walking and climbing is exhausting."

By the north side of the landing, they found a towering triangular-shaped archway eight metres high, but the opening had been caved in with cracked rocks and boulders.

Turtle shone his light next to the archway and revealed a gap in the ground. Not the kind of smooth, cylindrical hole one could easily slip into.

Syra's forehead creased. She clasped her chest, and she stared at the craggy opening. *What if I get stuck? What if something happens to Blaze or Turtle?* She felt pressure building at the base of her skull. *Could I find the exit out of this place?*

"This small opening is the first 'squeeze'," Turtle said, giving them a smug grin.

"Watch it." Blaze's voice elevated as he fed his feet into the hole. "It's a four-metre drop." With a push, he slid and disappeared inside the opening.

Tion aimed his light at the hole for Turtle, and the young man squeezed through after his brother.

Syra patted her damp forehead with her sleeve and forced herself to the hole's rim. She could see Turtle shining his light up at the hole. She dangled her feet over the edge, and inhaling a deep breath, she dropped herself into the opening with a yelp. Her feet thumped to the ground, and the jolt of the impact shot up her shins and into her knees.

The brothers flashed their lights and illuminated the broad lower chamber before them. Upon the light-grey walls appeared a meticulously carved frieze depicting the events of what seemed to be an ancient battle.

Syra pointed to the wall. "These carvings show the Kynorians and the Národan defending a tall entrance with weapons, but what are those *things* they're fighting?" She studied the fangs and claws of the beasts charging at the allied forces upon the wall. Her gut tightened at the sight of the depicted monsters, and she felt her heart thumping.

Blaze stood next to her and gazed at the artwork. "Those things look like a Denkarian crossed with a wolf and . . . a troll?"

With an echoing cry above them, Kardia came diving feet first through the hole. She slammed onto the ground like a sack of wet sand. Clasping her wrist, she wailed.

Tion's light jittered as he descended into the lower chamber after her. "What happened?" He raced to Kardia's side.

"I think my wrist is sprained." Kardia supported her limp hand.

"Syra, look at her wrist," Tion demanded, ushering Kardia to her. "She'll need to splint it."

Syra's heart was beating so heavily it felt like it would burst. She had underestimated the effort needed to prolong her lie. She saw the pain in Kardia's misty eyes. Staring at Kardia's hand, she noticed the swelling bruise developing from the base of her thumb to her lower forearm.

A wave of thoughts burned through Syra's mind. She shot her glance at Blaze and squeezed her fist tightly. *It's Blaze's fault I'm in this situation. A quick detour, they said.* She felt like strangling him. *Curse you, Blaze and your halfwit brother.*

"Do you think it's broken?" Tion's voice cut her vengeful thought stream.

Syra spun around and unlatched the healer's satchel. Fumbling inside, she found the small container labelled *Bandages*. Gauze bandages, elastic bandages, rigid straps, and triangular bandages were colour coded. Without the slightest clue, she grabbed a blue-coloured rigid strap. She lifted her eyes to find Turtle hovering his head above her.

"I think you want to use an elastic bandage." Turtle picked up the white bandage and slipped it inside her grip. "Elastic bandages are generally for sprains. The wrapping instructions are on the rear of the packaging," he whispered and winked at her.

"Yeah, I know." Syra ripped the bandage from his fingers. "You're not stupid after all," she whispered to him, feeling momentarily relieved.

She flipped the bandage and saw the four-part diagram of the instructions to wrap an ankle. *How different could a wrist be to wrap?* She peeled the tie from the dressing with her teeth and faced Kardia.

Syra's hands trembled as she reached for Kardia's wrist. Her neck felt clammy. Without a word, she slowly wrapped Kardia's wrist in a noticeably uneven version of the ankle diagram.

"Hold the bandage, Turtle," Syra directed him. "I'll get the strapping tape."

"The elastic hooks are better." Turtle pointed to a side pocket inside the healer's satchel.

Kardia groaned and muttered to Syra. "Do you know what you're doing?"

Syra fired her hardened glance at Turtle before delving into the satchel. She felt her forehead and neck heating, and she felt sweat beading on her cheek.

Turtle wrapped the end of the bandage onto Kardia's lower wrist. Syra fastened the elastic hooks onto the bandage and forced her smile at Kardia. "How does your hand feel now, Kardia?" she asked.

Kardia gently rubbed her bound wrist. "It's better, but I can still feel it throbbing."

"Do you think it's broken?" Tion asked Syra.

Syra aimed her gaze at Turtle, who shook his head slightly. "I don't think it's broken," she answered.

"Sprains are worse than a break," Turtle added. "We should wrap it in a sling. Keep the wrist elevated. Soft-tissue injuries take longer to heal than fractured bones."

Syra grimaced. "Just what I was thinking." *I hope you keep your mouth shut, Turtle.* She held her glare at him.

Turtle assisted her with wrapping Kardia's arm in a sling and strapping it across her shoulder with a triangular bandage he removed from his backpack.

"What are we going to do now?" Kardia asked. "We can't go back the way we came unless one of you brought a ladder."

"She's right." Tion flashed his light at Blaze. "How much farther?"

The young man's face tightened and went pale. "We're halfway through," Blaze told him.

Tion checked his watch. "It's been twenty-five minutes, and we're only halfway through?"

"Follow me." Blaze turned and strode to the end of the lower chamber.

After trekking half a kilometre upon an inclining passage, they arrived at a great chamber sixty metres across and fifteen metres in height. A warm flux of air streamed across Syra's face. A two-metre-wide water channel flowed steadily through the chamber's centre, slushing and trickling. Metre-wide, triangular pillars with carved glyphs joined the floor to the ceiling.

Blaze and Turtle jogged to the end of the chamber and waited for them.

"I don't remember seeing this." Blaze pointed at a crude hole in the wall.

"Neither do I." Turtle faced his brother and frowned.

"Oh, I hope you're not lost," Syra barked at them.

Tion shone his lamp at Blaze. "What's wrong now?"

Blaze pressed his hand against the outer edge of the hole. "We only remember two lead-off openings at the end of the second chamber." He aimed his light at the two archways on the nearby wall. "We haven't seen this one before."

They shone their lamps at the jagged mouth of the hole, which opened into a dark, serpentine tunnel. Syra noticed the freshly pulverised rocks strewn below it.

Folding into her anxieties as the claustrophobic essence of the subterranean province set in, Syra stared into the deep blackness of the hole. She imagined the long-forgotten evils of local legends and the malevolent forces which claimed the desolate underworld. She had to force herself away from the hole and its frightening yet intoxicating lure.

"Blaze, Turtle," Tion said, "keep to the path you know."

They entered the first archway on the left, one after another, except for Syra, who lingered behind. The dank and earthy scent of wet stone filled her mouth. A faint sound echoed inside the hole, like a long whisper. She stepped away. It felt like the darkness was calling for her. Inviting her to its embrace. Like the enchantment of a perplexing magic trick, she was drawn closer. Strangely enough, some part of her wanted to leap in.

CHAPTER 5

MYSTERIES OF THE SHADOW AGE

Syra inhaled a slow breath and exhaled her apprehension and her fears. The echoed voices of the company trailed away from her as she held her gaze into the shadows of the opening.

She felt her analytical mind reel her to the present time. Inching away from the hole, she turned and marched across the threshold to rejoin the group inside the tunnel.

"This entire mine, in the ancient times," Turtle said, "was wide enough to drive transporters through from one end to the other."

"One day the underground changed," Blaze added, "and areas of the tunnels caved in, blocking most of the major pathways."

"The mortal men and women," Tion said, "had little interest in the past. Such knowledge was either suppressed or scattered and obfuscated within the tomes of esoteric libraries. Especially the history of the Dura Mines.

Kardia smiled. "You know a lot about this place."

Blaze slapped his brother's shoulder. "What's the name of that Národ fellow Father knew?"

"He didn't know him," Turtle complained, "he just met him a couple of times."

"Yeah, alright. What's his name?"

"Demir," Turtle muttered.

"What?" Blaze squinted.

Turtle raised his voice. "His name is Demir."

Syra smiled. "Your arguments entertain me." She then frowned, feeling empty as she recalled her trivial disputes with Telora.

"Demir told Father," Blaze said, "the Kynorians left the mines because something bad was about to happen, but the Národan wouldn't leave so easily. The Národan got wealthy from the mines and wanted to continue working here. Demir said, 'Their desire transformed to greed, and their greed led to their fall'."

Turtle nudged Syra. "My father once said, Gloriatar, the High King of the Kynorians, and Manâzil, Prince of the Národan, were the co-architects of the Dura Mines. Rumours spread about an evil awakened deep within the mines."

"I remember this story," Blaze continued. "Gloriatar begged Manâzil to leave, but other forces were at work. Manâzil strove to increase the wealth of his father's empire in the northwest, so he continued his work in the mines.

"According to history, it was a hard parting for Gloriatar, as his friendship with Manâzil had been long and enduring. A doom had overcome Manâzil and his Národan miners. Soon the Národan who refused to exit the mines were never seen on the surface again."

"What bad thing happened down here?" Syra wondered.

Turtle shone his light at her. "I don't know, but some say this place was overrun by monsters, savage beasts of the underworld."

Syra remembered the carvings of the bestial creatures on the lower chamber wall. Doubt shrouded her.

"That's an old wife's tale," Kardia stated.

"If you say so," Blaze said.

"Beasts? Monsters?" Syra muttered. "I hope it's not true."

Kardia shot a rigid glance at Turtle. "That's the last thing we need to hear, walking underground with no immediate exit."

Tion pushed Blaze and Turtle forward. "Enough bedtime stories, you two."

After four hundred metres, the brothers slowed their pace as the path inclined, and the walls narrowed until they met at a gap in the wall. The opening was three hand spans wide.

Blaze wriggled his arm from the strap of his pack. "You'll need to remove your backpacks before entering this part." He squeezed into the crevice.

"I drag it behind like this." Turtle entered after Blaze, dangling his pack by his side.

One by one, they entered the narrow gap. Moving with shuffling steps, they progressed until they arrived at a long hall.

Syra could see the pillared façade of a concaved passage by the end of the hall. Through the dusty lamplight, she gazed at the ten carved Národan faces recessed upon the ivory-coloured marble façade. A singular Národan rune was placed above each head. The sight of their grim, fierce faces caused her to sigh, and she felt their piercing eyes penetrate her soul.

Blaze glanced at his compass. "I know we're behind, but we're heading along the correct path at least." He panned his light into the passage. "Good news is we're more than halfway through now."

Tion caressed Kardia's head.

Syra smiled and exhaled in relief for the first time down there. *Finally, a way out of this cavern.*

"Follow me." Blaze crossed the threshold and strode along the path.

Syra noticed the marble walls on either side were smeared with swirls of red ochre and mud. The crassly scratched patterns covered the root-like veins of the marble, and scattered about them were the prints of clawed hands.

"Primordial cave art," Tion remarked, aiming his lamp at the wall as he marched.

"Did the Kynorians do this?" Syra asked, gawking at the mess.

"No," Tion answered quickly. "Neither the Kynorians nor the Národan would defile their kingdom like this."

Tion's words ruptured the fragile layer of Syra's courage, exposing the surface of her evolving anxieties. It seemed the underworld offered the marvels of the past civilisation. At the same time, it volunteered a dark, shrouded agitation.

Syra felt the ground beneath her feet soften along the winding passage as the terrain's surface changed into muddy soil. The path inclined to a set of steps eight metres in width. Forcing her leaden legs into motion, she leaped up and counted twenty steps before arriving at the final tread.

In the corridor ahead of her, she saw pendant lighting fashioned from what appeared to be gold dangling from the high ceiling. The lighting fixtures trailed into the distance as far as she could see. A cracked circular pillar was strewn about the ground, and the company weaved through its thick blocks.

"Ah, can you smell that?" Syra covered her mouth and nose.

An acidic biological reek cut through the air, and she watched Kardia cover her mouth with her shirt.

Tion gave Blaze a nervous stare.

"Don't be alarmed," Blaze assured them, "there are all kinds of smells down here."

"Awful," Syra mumbled, trying to hold her breath and walk simultaneously.

Tion called to them. "Wait." His voice was sharp. He panned his lamp to the left. There came a bright flicker, which glinted in his light. "Over there." He raced to the shining object. They rushed after him.

Tion squatted and collected an item of clothing from the ground.

Syra stared at the new coat in Tion's grip and could not understand how it arrived at such a remote part of the land. A forbidden realm few in their days had seen.

"We don't usually find blue coats down here," Blaze said, pointing at the coat in Tion's hand.

"Small enough for a petite girl." Tion handed it to Kardia.

"Looks like it's in good condition." Kardia shone her light on the circular brooch pinned on the left breast side.

Syra smelt a familiar and distinct fragrance wafting from the coat. *Spice and rosewater perfume.* She stared at the label on the jacket. Her heart raced, and she could not control its pulsing rhythm. *Purchased from Grandinem Central. Small enough for a petite girl.*

The cool air closed in on her. A memory of the girl wearing the coat flashed in her mind. She shivered as her final thought seeped into her soul. Her upper lip trembled.

"Syra, what's wrong?" Kardia leaned closer.

"The coat." Syra sniffled. "It belongs to my sister. It's the one I bought for her last winter." Her voice choked. She glanced at Kardia. "By the way, I'm not a healer. Your path seemed logical because I needed a way to find my sister."

Turtle pointed his finger at her and smiled. "I knew you weren't."

Tion shook his head and frowned, giving Syra a poisonous stare. Kardia's eyes bulged at her. Blaze scoffed and smirked.

Clasping the scented coat in her hand, Syra felt her shame slowly dissolve, exposing the arrogance she knew was her most unique survival mechanism. "Don't you give me that look!" she snapped at Tion. "Marius wouldn't have let me come. Besides, you don't know what it's like to lose the only person you have."

"You shouldn't have lied," Tion said. "What if one of us gets seriously hurt down here? You could compromise the safety of the entire group. Not to mention the fiasco Marius will be entangled in if we go missing."

"Safety, you say?" Syra crept closer to Tion. "We're in a desolate cave half a kilometre below the surface. Carvings of clawed beasts and faces of ancient warriors cover the walls. I'm tired, sore, and it stinks down here." She stabbed her finger into Blaze's chest. "He said we'd be out of this place in twenty-five minutes."

Kardia pushed between them, placing her hand on Tion's shoulder, and faced Syra. "Ease up. We're obviously on the right track, and with some luck, we can find the missing students."

"This route." Tion's voice echoed inside the passage. "It's completely against Grandinem Academy protocol. They shouldn't have come here." He kicked at the dusty floor. "The Academy must be punished for this transgression. If they knew about it, someone is getting locked away in the dungeons of Alakritas."

"What if they didn't know about it?" Kardia asked.

"No." Tion shook his head. "Someone must have known about this. Someone must have led them into these mines, and that person must have extensive knowledge of this area. The Denkarian Elites might have a hand in this."

Syra felt the rushing streams of anxiety storming through her. "I think you're right, Tion. "Maybe they were led down here."

Syra stared at the troubled faces of her companions. She saw the dark patches around Turtle's eyes, and she glanced at Blaze's twitching grip on his backpack straps. Tion and Kardia stood beside each other. Their sweaty faces were smeared in doubt and shame. The lamp light cast ominous shadows against the walls as the threat of the Dura Mines crept slowly inside Syra's soul.

Syra gazed into Tion's eyes. "We are not prepared to enter these abandoned Mines."

CHAPTER 6
EVISCERATED DISCOVERY

IN THE EMPTY SILENCE, they gazed at Syra. The chains of her reactive mind dragged her into the darker recesses of subconsciousness, where harmful thoughts have the power to destroy a person.

She gripped the material of her pants with her sweaty fingers. Her arms and shoulders tensed as she squeezed her muscles like a braid of clumped wires. The constant sound of dripping water only added to her agitation. In the absence of the sun, the claustrophobia of the underworld was beginning to smother her reality. Syra flinched away from her mental haze.

Tion broke the silence. "We'll search this area." He shone his lamp on the edge of the chamber. "Check the walls and the ground but don't go too far."

Following his orders, the group dispersed through the twenty-metre by forty-metre chamber. Their lamps illuminated the compartmentalised rooms and archways along the south wall.

Turtle leaped upon a small marble ledge and surveyed

the eastern walls, panning his light along each corner and crevice.

Syra shone her lamp at the ceiling and noticed brown palm-sized clumps scattered across the ceiling. *Maybe that's where the awful smell is coming from.*

Kardia shouted, "Footprints over here." She aimed her lamp at the ground in the middle of the chamber.

"They're not ours." Tion pointed at the unknown impressions.

"Since we entered," Kardia said, "the ground has been mostly flat, hard surfaces, but this thin layer of micro-soil makes it easier to see the prints."

"What size shoe does your sister wear?" Tion asked Syra.

"Most of her shoes are size seven," Syra replied, staring at the impression. "Seems like a lot of mixed footprints, though. Could they have split up?"

"It would be foolish to separate down here," Tion said, "especially with a group of inexperienced students. None of this makes sense."

Syra pointed her light to the left. "Look at those marks on the wall." She saw linear scratches on the wall as if someone had used the surface to sharpen a tool.

"These scratches look out of place," Kardia said, "just like the wall marks we saw earlier."

Turtle cried from the other side of the chamber, flagging them to his side. Upon the floor, there appeared to be a clump of flesh.

Kardia bent her knees. "These are decayed remains covered in . . ."

"Is that blood?" Syra shouted, jumping to the side.

The sight and smell of the rotting clump made her dry retch. The fetor was so intense she spun away. Blocking her nose, she took shallow breaths through her mouth. She dared to look across her shoulder.

The crimson viscera gleamed in Tion's light. "It's certainly blood."

Blaze and Turtle covered their mouths with their hands.

Kardia stared at the clump from both sides. "Hard to tell whether it's animal or human. It seems to be intestinal tissue."

"Turtle," Tion demanded, "take your brother and scan the path ahead. Find out where these footprints lead. We'll wait for you here."

The brothers careered along the corridor, thumping the ground with leaping strides.

Kardia's forehead creased. "These footprints appear to be deeper and slightly misshapen." She measured the depth of the prints with her finger.

Syra frowned. "You seem troubled by that."

Kardia squinted. "For reasons I don't know. It just doesn't add up."

Syra could see the cogs in Kardia's scientific mind turning, and her full lips moved as if she was mumbling to herself. The animal specialist seemed confused about the anomaly. Syra felt sick in her stomach, but she stood by silently as Kardia twisted this way and that, gazing at the mass of flesh.

Kardia kicked away the hand-sized stone next to the clump granting her a side angle of view.

Kardia's doubt and the trailing stench left Syra more than nauseated. She felt her stomach squirming, and her mouth began to salivate, the kind of dampness before you vomit. With a groaning cough, Syra twisted away from them, folded over, and spewed onto the ground.

"Syra." Tion rushed to her side.

Kardia rubbed Syra's shoulders. "It's the stench, isn't it?"

Syra nodded as she reached for her water canister and rinsed her mouth, spitting the water onto the ground. She inhaled a deep breath as the urge to retch again subsided.

"This smell is toxic," Kardia said.

"We must leave this place." Tion stared into Kardia's eyes. "Tell me, what doesn't add up here? Are there any indicators suggesting this clump of flesh is human?"

"The flesh appears to be human," Kardia replied, "because of the redness of the surrounding muscle tissue. In the same light, it doesn't look human. I'd know. I've dissected many animals and seen enough cadavers to last a lifetime."

Syra wiped her mouth and stood with her hands clasping the back of her head.

Kneeling closer, Tion gyrated his lamp. "It must be animal, then?"

"It appears to be hominid by its movements." Kardia pointed to a secondary set of adjacent marks on the ground. "Look here. Handprints and knuckle prints, but they're not as prevalent. Whatever it is, it used its hands partially for movement."

"Could they be apes?" Syra asked.

Kardia glanced up at her with a rigid stare. "Apes don't live this far underground."

Syra's inner ear rang, and her foggy breath wafted across her lamplight. She recalled an old verse poem. *The truth is a merciless executioner of a lie, and it can never be taken away. That which kills the lie will set you free.*

Kardia pointed to the print. "The three-arch system is associated with human feet, not apes."

"If it's not human," Syra asked Kardia, "and if it's not an ape, what exactly is it?"

"An extinct hominid species, maybe," Kardia answered. "Some of the fringe archaeologists, the people the Academy hates, would speak of an alternately evolved hominid species that terrorised the northwestern lands. They claimed it was in the distant past, but who knows if it's true."

Staring at the imprint, Syra envisioned the type of bipedal beast that would live underground. Ropey limbs and hunched torso. A gnarled, misshaped head. Sharp canines. Protruding tusks. Black eyes and a network of purple veins branching over a pale-skinned body. *Anything that lives in this dark place must be evil.* An aching sense of dread smothered her soul.

In the cavern's silence, a rattling of vocalised noises reverberated through the corridor and into the chamber.

Raahhhhh, harrhhh, raashhh.

Syra clung to Kardia's arm. Tion spun and panned his light across the compartments of the chamber.

"What was that?" Syra whispered.

Kardia stood with erect shoulders. The echoing diminuendo of the sounds fell into silence.

Tion quickly aimed his light at the opposite end of the corridor.

The pounding of rushing feet thumped the ground along the southern wing of the corridor. Syra froze on her feet. With tensed shoulders, she awaited the worst.

"Hey!" Turtle yelled.

The brothers' lights wobbled erratically against the walls as they careered toward them.

Syra exhaled and sighed. "You scared the life from me."

"We found something." Blaze came to a halt. He breathed short, quick breaths. "One hundred metres up the passage." He held in his hand the remains of a damaged red journal, silver-bound, with the initials *Mr B* on the front cover. He handed the journal to Tion. The pages were slightly damp and covered in dirt.

Raashhh, kokokoko, kekekeke.

Another bizarre set of sounds bounced along the walls and into the chamber. The hairs on Syra's chilled arms stood on end. She clenched her fists and peered into the darkness.

Turtle broke the silence with a whisper. "We heard that same sound earlier."

"Switch off all the lamps," Tion demanded, keeping his lamp on.

They huddled together in the bleak gloom of the single lamplight.

Kardia took the journal and opened it to the first page. Tion held his lamp above it. The white pages had yellowed in the dampness of the mines. Syra saw the slight tremor in Kardia's hands, adding to her own fear.

Kardia read the journal in a lowered voice. "It's an account of events," she said. "*Day One* is marked at the top of the page, but many pages are ripped out. Then it continues to *Day Three*." She turned the soiled pages. "*Inside . . . horrible sounds growling head.* No, *heard.* The next few words are missing; *shapes move below.* The next part is blotted out with a dark substance. Can't tell what the substance is. I think the next bit is *taken them d.* D for down, I assume? Then, *we are the last alive.* The next page has been torn away. On the following page is the word *buranith,* scribbled toward the bottom."

"What's *buranith* mean?" Turtle asked.

Syra gazed at Kardia in the hope of a logical, academic explanation. She could see the strain on Kardia's face.

Kardia glanced at Turtle before returning her eyes to the journal. "It's a root word for bipedal animals, but it's a very ancient word that's only used by specialists on the fringe. It sounds like a Kynorian word."

"What's after *buranith*?" Tion moved the lamp closer to the page.

Kardia flipped to the next page. "It reads, *are in here,* and then, *we can't see, but only hear them surround us.*"

Syra tilted her head to see along the corridor. Her fingers trembled so forcefully that she clenched her hands into fists.

Blaze and Turtle stood like a couple of skittish children, darting their eyes about the chamber.

"We shouldn't have taken this route," Syra whispered to Turtle. Her gleaming eyes were gall. Her words were threatening, and she watched Blaze and Turtle bow their heads. "Not so confident now, are you, Blaze?"

The brothers made no sound.

Syra faced Tion and Kardia. "How could an abandoned mine be safe?" She held her gaze at them.

Kardia handed the journal to Tion. "We'll be fine."

Tion pinched the corners of the last few pages and turned them, but nothing was written. He flipped to the final page. "Wait . . ."

In the darkness, the lamplight revealed his widened eyes. His mouth moved, but he made no sound. He adjusted the light on angles, checking the pages.

"What's wrong?" Kardia asked him.

Tion stood there, glued to the same page. His face went pale, and he shook his head.

Kardia's voice grew louder. "What's wrong?"

Tion lifted his gaze to Kardia. "The foul smells. The blue coat. The clump of flesh and blood. The footprints. This damaged Academy journal." Drops of sweat trickled upon Tion's temples and onto his cheeks as he glanced at Syra. "The group of students who entered this mine never left."

"What does it say?" Kardia demanded.

Syra panted forcefully. She felt her lungs pushing against her ribcage as she inhaled the stagnant cavern air. She cowered inside the light reflecting off the journal's page.

Tion whispered, *"Do not enter the mines."*

CHAPTER 7
THE HORDE UNLEASHED

Syra snatched the journal from Tion's hand. She could hear Turtle's heavy breathing behind her left ear.

Her vision was locked onto the five faded words scribbled on the pale page. Her dry throat felt scratchy as she swallowed, and she had never feared five words more than those. As a dissident who had always scraped her way through life, she had never faced such a harrowing circumstance.

Syra recalled the time she was accosted and thrown to the ground by Denkarian soldiers in a lane outside Epion City. Resistance rallies organised by the Firekites often ended in participants being rounded up, beaten, and sometimes killed. She rolled her aching shoulder, which had never been the same since that altercation. After terrorising her, the soldiers let her off with a warning. Beneath Númaria's surface, would there be a warning?

"I pity the owner of this journal," Tion said. "Whoever it was, their words unnerve me."

Kardia glanced at Tion. "The dangers of the mines have resurrected from ages past."

Turtle switched his lamp on and shone it along the passage from which they had entered the chamber. His upper lip was damp, and the hand clasping the lamp was shaky.

Syra stared at Blaze's creased brow, and she felt his arrogance diminish with the words of the journal entry. Shadows covered Kardia's anaemic face in the lamplight. Tion's bloodshot eyes were glazed yet focused as he hunched his shoulders, exuding the distress he appeared to be suffering.

A quaking thump shuddered the floor beneath their feet. The company stumbled, and the aftershock permeated the mines drizzling debris from cracks in the chamber's ceiling. A wrenching noise swirled from beyond the walls, not a sharp piercing sound but more like the dull splintering of a tree trunk under a pressurised torsion.

Syra gasped and clamped the journal shut with her hands. Tion yanked Kardia's arm, shoved the brothers toward the near wall, and guided Syra after them.

With their backs pressed against the pitted stone wall, Tion switched his lamp off.

Above the rapid breathing of Blaze and Turtle, Syra could hear the rasps of her own wavering breaths as she anxiously inhaled and exhaled. *If there's a Númarian quake, we're all dead down here.*

When the last tremor subsided, Syra focused on the distant clatter. As she studied the noises, what seemed like a rapid succession of short, sharp knocking sounds transformed into the throated vocal calls of an abrasive, humanoid voice.

In her fear and confusion, Syra reached her hand along the wall. "Kardia, is that you?" she whispered.

"Yes, it's me." Kardia clasped Syra's hand.

"Did you hear that?" Syra asked her.

Tion switched his lamp on and smothered the light to emit a soft glow.

They huddled around Tion's light. Another tremor rumbled along the parallel passages and into the chamber. A low cracking noise swept along the paths, providing a stir in the cavern's deep. The looming aura of the Dura Mines came alive.

Syra fell to her knees and began to hyperventilate. She opened the top of her pack and retrieved her water canister. *I don't want to die here, not like this.*

She coughed on the water as she drank, spilling it on her chin and jacket.

Kardia placed her hand on Syra's shoulder. "We'll find the exit."

Syra ignored her sentiment, stuffed her hand inside her pack, and clasped her knife. She fastened the blade to her belt. Her experience wielding a knife was limited to chopping up vegetables and carving into cooked meats. Syra cast the useless healing satchel to the side, stuffed the journal inside her backpack, and then forced herself to her feet.

Tion yanked Blaze by his lapel. "Get us out of here." His grating voice echoed in the chamber, and he removed his hand from the lamp light.

Harrhhh raashhh, kokokoko kekekeke.

The booming tremors duplicated from beyond the walls of the chamber, and it sounded like an ogrish beast was hammering the foundations of the mines.

Blaze flicked his lamp on. "This way," he yelled, speeding to the northern passageway.

Turtle rushed after him. Tion, Kardia, and Syra chased the brothers, skidding across the chamber's path.

A bellowing thump shook the ground. Syra felt it

through her heels and into her thighs. The mines trembled and boomed twice more. A long searing shriek rose from beyond the walls, so loud Syra felt its vibrations against her chest.

Shaarrrrrhhhhh.

The chilling sound ricocheted off the walls. Blaze and Turtle dashed along the corridor.

After two hundred metres, the floor inclined into a ramp leading to a five-metre-wide concaved tunnel.

Split-level pathways and lanes opened on both sides of the tunnel, falling into forgotten chambers with life-size statues inside marble niches. Turtle waited for Syra at the top of the ramp. Tion ushered Kardia as she cradled her damaged wrist.

They sprinted along the tunnel, chasing Blaze's vibrating light. The smooth marble walls were ruined with deep gashes and swirling red patterns.

"Keep running," Tion shouted.

Syra's legs felt numb with the dump of adrenalin gushing through her veins. Her lungs surged. She pumped her arms, trailing at the rear of the group.

"I'm sorry," Turtle said with a shaky voice. "We shouldn't have come this way."

Syra heard vocalised snarling and grunting to her left, not like a predacious wolf hunting her, but more like a tribal war cry. The edges of her light caught a large shadow fleeing against the pillars of an adjacent passage. *Keep running.* She forced herself.

A gurgling bark issued from a lane on the opposite side of the tunnel. Foul smells spewed into her lungs. A rasping screech cut above her right ear. She panted and thrashed her arms.

Another wailing screech reverberated behind her until a

clamour of throated sounds sprang through the multiple chambers and passages.

The harsh voices were chesty, and some were placed in the throat, similar to a human but more like the belching and barking of a hound. She noticed the voices were communicative in their percussive patterns.

Speeding on tired feet, she coughed on her thick saliva as her lungs burned inside her chest.

"Syra!" Turtle yelled. "Behind you."

A raging growl shot above her, and she felt the strike of a blunt force hit the back of her head. Her legs gave out, and she fell, skidding on her belly and her hands across the cold floor.

She spat the grainy dust from her mouth and crawled to the nearest wall. Her grazed knuckles and fingers stung, and her hands and head throbbed. Her eyes flickered, and she sank prostrate onto the tunnel's floor into a daze.

The rest of them continued sprinting up the tunnel as the floor beneath them began to fall at a ten-degree angle.

After a few minutes, Tion slowed his pace and glanced over his shoulder. "Syra!" he yelled. "Turtle . . ."

Kardia and Blaze slowed their pace.

"Where are they?" Kardia aimed her light along the tunnel.

"I thought they were behind you," Tion said.

"Why are you stopping?" Blaze shouted, forty metres ahead of them.

"Your brother and Syra are missing," Tion told him, wiping the sweat from his face.

The passage fell silent, all except for their heavy breathing. Tion scanned the rippled passage walls with his light. Still, the beam of light only illuminated the glinting dust particles wafting across the tunnel nearby.

"We have to go back." Blaze marched along the path.

"Wait for a moment." Tion held him back. "Something's down here, and we don't know what it is."

Blaze slapped his hand away. "I'm going to find my brother." He leaped into a jog and hurried along the passage.

"What about Syra?" Kardia shouted after him.

"We have no weapons and no exit," Tion told her. "Whatever is down here has claimed the students; worse still, they know these paths and passages better than any of us do."

"What's your suggestion, then?" she asked.

"We find the exit," he whispered harshly, peering into her eyes.

Kardia slowly shook her head. She flinched as she slipped her damaged hand from the sling.

"What are you doing?" Tion enquired.

"I'll need both hands to find Syra!" She turned and sped back along the path.

CHAPTER 8
TERRORS OF THE DURA MINES

SYRA FORCED HER EYES OPEN. She gently caressed the burning pain that fired from the back of her head to the nape of her neck. Damp to the touch. She pinched her fingers and realised it was not sweat. With blurred vision, she saw her lamp on the floor near the far wall, its light aimed into an adjacent lane.

Syra could see many metre-high pillars along each of the lanes. Atop each pillar were bowls filled with glinting gems.

Diamond-shaped lamps of the derelict lighting system upon the walls reflected the light from her lamp.

She groaned as she lifted herself to her knees. Glancing to the right, she listened to the obscure echoes rising and falling into the passage she had come from.

The scent of damp soil whirled into her nostrils. Snarls and gurgling sounds sprang from the ramp on the opposite side of the tunnel, made by the same primitive voice she heard earlier in the chamber. A popping and clicking noise issued from beyond the foundations she hid behind.

Kekekekeke, Kokokokoko.

She inhaled a short breath and froze. She wanted to move, but the arcane sounds kept her frozen in a position like a startled animal caught in a hunter's light.

The noises blared again and tumbled into the tunnel, but this time they were closer. Much closer.

A painful strain fired from her shoulder to her chest as she forced herself up from the floor, pressing her shoulders against the cold wall.

"Ah-hh! No! Nah-hh . . ." Convulsive screams reverberated from a parallel pathway twenty metres in the distance.

"Turtle," Syra whispered.

She flinched at a sudden cracking, which stifled her breath. Not a rupturing sound, more like the splintering burst of a voracious thylacine crunching through bone. The sound trailed along the passage. Multiple grunts and snarls along the paths brought the underworld alive.

Syra inhaled a sharp breath and clasped her mouth. She could feel her hand shaking as the tumultuous clamour injected her soul with a terror she could barely withstand.

Turtle's wailing screams rang into the clearing. The agony in his voice peaked until it reached a primal ecstasy that spilled into every crevice of the mines.

Amid Turtle's awful yelping, Syra heard him crying his brother's name in vain, sputtering amid his pleas for the savagery to stop. His agonising bellows tore through every inch of her soul, and she felt her heart smashing her ribcage from the inside.

In a hazardous attempt to aid Turtle, Syra marched two steps forward before a loud shriek issued from a side lane, causing her to leap back to the wall. She wanted to help him, but her shameful fear suppressed what little courage she could muster. What malevolent creatures lurked in the mines?

The macabre ferocity of his final cry reverberated along the passage. Syra winced as she pressed herself hard up against the wall. Turtle's forlorn wailing would be forever branded into her mind.

Squeezing her eyes shut, she covered her mouth to prevent herself from heaving as Turtle's final torturous scream was severed into a swift silence.

With her shoulders pinned to the wall, she dared to open her eyes. Syra's hands trembled, and she gripped the blade's handle, still strapped to her hip. Deep inside her heart, she knew she had no courage to save Turtle. *What a coward I am to sit here and do nothing. No ... I'm a survivor, and survivors do whatever it takes to stay alive.*

Such justified cowardice stripped away her sanity, and she sank into a pang of shadowy guilt. *Is this what I've become?*

Syra felt a pulsating vibration against her back. The pulses were rhythmic, like the tapping cadence of a four-count pattern. Staring over her shoulder, she noticed an orange glow emanating from her backpack. Syra fed her arms from the straps and placed the pack on the ground.

Unlatching the bag, she was surprised to find the transparent Kynorian axe she had taken from the weighing station fully illuminated in soft orange and blue lights. As she lifted the axe from the backpack, it flashed white light. The light dimmed, and a hologram appeared above the head of the axe, featuring the Kynorian script she had seen on the megalith outside.

Unable to read the ancient Kynorian script, she followed the hologram as it played motion images in sequence. A depiction of the axe's anatomy showed its attributes. The hologram displayed an armour-clad Kynorian warrior slicing the arm of what appeared to be a clawed beast, similar to the wall depictions in the lower chamber.

The hologram displayed a sequence of events showing the beast's upper arm and chest freezing.

This axe is capable of Frost Damage, she thought, *freezing anything it slices.* She twisted it in her hand, inspecting the blue, glowing symbols on the blade and handle. It appeared as if the axe knew she needed assistance.

The next set of holographic images showed the axe glowing orange when the monsters were nearby. More images flowed, detailing an array of other creatures and beasts the axe would detect. Some of the creatures were quadrupedal, as tall as a great panthera, while others were bipedal and reptile-like.

A hologram of white and blue waves representing sound revealed the monsters' capabilities to echolocate and measure pressure changes within the underground.

According to the detailed holograms, the beast's nocturnal senses could detect arrhythmia, increased blood pressure, oestrous in females, and aldehyde, the organic compound that gives blood its metallic scent.

Can these monsters smell my blood?

She touched the back of her stinging, damp head and gasped. The blood had streamed along her neck and spine, soaking the top of her shirt.

Resting the axe against the wall, she quickly unlatched the front pocket of her pack and retrieved a small spray bottle labelled *Citrus Bloom*. Syra kept this disinfecting, anti-viral healing oil on her everywhere she travelled. She peeled her handkerchief from her pocket. Closing her eyes and biting her lip, she sprayed the citrus mist onto the back of her head.

The sting took her breath away, shooting the searing

pain into her jaw and temples. Her eyes teared and she sighed. Syra sprayed her handkerchief, wiped the excess blood from her head, and discarded it to the side of the tunnel.

Collecting the frost axe, she examined the glowing inscription upon the handle. When she swiped her finger atop the first symbol of the inscription, the hologram suddenly collapsed.

She slung her backpack across her shoulder. With the radiating light from the axe, she ambled to her lamp on the opposite side of the tunnel.

She crept along the path with the axe in her shivering right hand and the lamp in her left hand, hoping she would see the daylight again.

Tion's head throbbed. He hurtled along the passageway, vaulting atop fallen pillars strewn across the pathway. Sweat dripped into his eyes as he traced Blaze's storming pace with his lamp in his shaking grasp. He heard Kardia's thumping footsteps and her swishing arms against her backpack behind him. Despite the adrenalin in his system, his legs began to burn. *How long can we last down here?*

Blaze slowed his fervent pace and came to a halt in the middle of the passage. Dusty particles glinted in the light shining from his lamp as he flashed the light at them.

Tion and Kardia slowed their pace until they came to a stop twenty metres behind him. A loud bark echoed through the tunnel, causing them to flinch. Panning their lights along the parallel lanes, Tion saw the shadow of an upright beast swiftly descend a ramp and disappear into the tunnel's blackness.

As Blaze's light flickered and switched off, a piercing screech soared at the end of the passage.

Tion reeled Kardia to his side, holding her closely. He felt her body quivering, and she clasped her damaged wrist. He ushered her behind the cracked column of a nearby wall.

Blaze groaned vehemently. "This lamp is faulty." He squeezed and smacked the lamp's base until the light shimmered and flashed back on.

Clicking and popping sounds of echolocation tolled into the adjacent paths, fading into the blackness. A faint scream rang in one of the distant chambers.

Blaze froze. "Turtle . . ." he muttered.

Dissonant shrieks hit the ceiling and trailed into the passage without warning. The ground rumbled with the trampling of heavily landed steps.

Tion aimed his lamp into the passage, and its rays illuminated the gnarled faces of monsters with grinding fangs and matted furs, rasping with their mouths agape.

"Go!" Blaze shouted.

Thrusting their arms and legs, they sprinted along the tunnel. Lamps jittered. Dust flicked into the air, and clamorous snarls crashed against the walls. Sweat seeped into Tion's eyes. He breathed heavily as he struggled to manoeuvre the many strewn boulders blocking the tunnel.

Leading at the front, Blaze dashed into a bend in the passage and onto a long corridor with an elevated, concave ceiling.

A hairy, seven-foot-tall quadrupedal beast with a short face and flared nostrils scurried across the path. Its glowing eyes glimmered in Blaze's light, and its burbling growls echoed along the adjacent passage.

"Blaze, the exit?" Tion shouted. His heart slammed in his chest.

"We're getting closer," Blaze yelled.

Tion slowed his pace and glanced over his shoulder.

"Kardia!" he yelled. "Kardia!" He skidded across the ground and flashed his lamp into the darkness.

The stabbing pain in his stomach felt like he was being torn apart from the inside. His glance darted from left to right in the hope of finding her. Creeping forward, Tion aimed his light onto a descending ramp connecting the corridor. He spun around, pointed his light at an alcove, and flinched to see a Národan statue beyond the wafting dust. He began puffing, and his hands trembled, shaking the lamplight about the corridor.

He stared at the small streams of sand falling from the cracks in the ceiling, but not all the sand in the world could fill the crack in his broken heart.

A cacophony of abrasive shrieks shot into the corridor. The piercing wail of Kardia's harsh voice fired into the hall like a pulse of rapid lightning.

"No. No!" He fumbled with his lamp. "Kardia!" Tion's palpitating voice sank pitifully into the dampened tunnel.

"Answer me!"

Abandoning his exit, Tion dashed to the origin of her voice. Into the void of blackness, deep inside the bowels of the mines, he pursued the vain hope of finding his beloved Kardia.

CHAPTER 9
SACRED LIGHT IN THE CAVERN'S DEEP

SYRA CREPT SILENTLY along the sloping pathway, glancing up at the obscuring mists that billowed overhead. In the after-shock of Turtle's torturous screams, it was as if the under-world had become freezing, stealing the warmth from inside her. After ten minutes, the cobblestone path wound and levelled before opening into a grand tunnel with a concaved ceiling.

For an instant, Syra felt as if time had ceased. Not because she had entered an old and derelict mine but because she had crossed into an alternate dimension of advancement she had never thought existed.

The eight-metre-wide tiled tunnel featured detailed carvings of Kynorian faces above the archway architraves. The faces appeared so accurate that Syra could not tell whether they were precisely fashioned art or Kynorians frozen inside the walls. At closer inspection, she noticed the faces had gleaming jewels as eyes, and some of the carvings had been vandalised.

The lower interior walls of the tunnel featured a dark-grey stripe flanked by gold geometric patterns stretching along the entire passage. Such symmetry gave it the opulent yet unwelcoming aura of a luxurious labyrinth.

The grand passage had served as the lifeblood of a thriving ancient city. As Syra slowed her pace, she felt the numbness in her legs dissipate. Taking controlled breaths, she ignored the stinging pain at the back of her head.

The walkway levelled, and she noticed a break in the wall thirty metres ahead. She lowered each foot softly and felt the crunch of crushed rocks beneath her feet. The taste of iron swelled in her throat.

Some innate force pulled her attention to the gap in the wall. Her heart throbbed heavily inside her chest. The shallowness of her breathing began to asphyxiate her. She inched closer to the crevice.

Syra directed her lamplight into the gap, and a sudden rush of cool air whipped her face.

A rugged grip clenched onto her forearm. She raised her axe.

"Hey, it's me." Blaze flashed his light at her.

Syra expelled a sigh of relief. "You imbecile. I nearly sliced your bloody arm off."

"Why do you have that axe?" Blaze questioned.

She lowered the axe, hiding it by her side in an attempt to divert him from questioning her as to why she had taken the weapon.

"Have you seen Turtle?" He grabbed her by the shoulders.

"Wait, where's Tion and Kardia?" She panned her gaze along the passage. "Where are the only logical people in our group?"

"They're gone," he said. "I heard Turtle's voice. Have you seen him?"

Her eyes locked onto his, and she froze. She tried to

answer him, but some force inside of her seized the words from passing her lips. She gave no reply and tilted her head away. The hard exhalation of his breath echoed along the pathway.

"What's going on down here?" His voice was choked up.

"You've led us into a pit." She spat her words at him. "This place is crawling with a pack of primitive, flesh-eating monsters. The ancient miners obviously knew about them, and that's why they abandoned the Dura Mines."

"Those were just stories," he told her in defence. "Stories to scare people like us from coming here." His mouth trembled. "This can't be happening." He placed both hands behind his head and paced up and down.

"Well, it is," she whispered loudly. "I could slap you right now for leading us down here."

Blaze faced her. "You must have been the last one to see Turtle."

She glanced up at him and did not say a word.

"Tell me what happened." His red face dripped with sweat, and his eyes were bloodshot in the light.

"Stop questioning me, Mister Mountaineer, and show me the exit."

He shook his head. "I'm not leaving this place without my brother."

"Did you listen to a word I said?" Syra barked at him. "Your brother is gone, just like Tion and Kardia. My sister is gone too. If you haven't been paying attention, your problem isn't greater than mine."

"You're a selfish girl, Syra, and what you lack in responsibility, you make up for in your arrogance."

"Listen, Blaze," she cried, "if two ancient races with advanced technologies vanished from their excavation sites, what hope did a group of young scientists have down here? Better still, what hope do we have?"

Blaze stood in the light of his lamp. Syra could see his hunched shoulders and the defeat in his eyes. *I pity you, Blaze.*

"What we should be doing instead of arguing," she told him, "is finding our way out. We can inform Marius and call for help. Now, where is this exit?" She smashed his shoulder with her fist.

Blaze stumbled and winced as he rubbed his shoulder.

He aimed his light into the corridor. "The exit isn't far. It's about three hundred metres along this winding passageway, and then it's a hard left turn. Follow me."

They dashed along the pathway as quietly as their feet would allow.

Syra's hands began to quiver, and her wound throbbed with all the running she had done. Her body was suddenly fighting a maelstrom of fear and emotions, which seemed to have no limit. She felt her sanity diminishing inside the dark underworld and was pained by the rash decision to abandon the search for her sister. She coughed the dust from her lungs and prayed she could feel the sun on her face once again.

She gasped as she stared at her frost axe radiating orange and vibrating in her grip. *The beasts are close.* She switched her light into the many ramps and lanes leading into the central passageway. *Nothing.*

Hammering footsteps echoed behind her.

Blaze increased his pace, leaping into a hasty jog forty metres ahead of her.

A bellowing roar shot into the corridor from a lane on the left side. A snarling monster lunged across the passageway, striking Blaze with a crude, spiked weapon.

Blaze yelped and dropped his lamp. Tumbling to the floor, he squealed and thrashed his body, clasping his knee.

Syra lifted the Kynorian axe and slowly crept to him. The sounds of the creatures diminished, and the corridor lay silent, except for Blaze's groaning and rasping.

He tried reaching for his lamp. "Syra, help." His fingertips barely touched it.

"Wait there," she cried, "I coming."

Syra aimed her light at the distant gurgling emanating from the lane to the left. She lowered her stance and aimed her light at Blaze, who was squirming in agony. Slowly she crept towards him. The axe vibrated heavily in her hand, but it beeped twice, and the axe blade flashed red.

Thumping feet hammered the ramp leading into the corridor. To her terror, a hairy beast with a humanoid face crawled on all fours, grunting and sniffing the ground just metres away from Blaze.

Scrambling quietly back to the wall, she halted to inch herself inside an alcove, barely wide enough to conceal her. *No . . . Blaze, get up.* She thought, staring at his imminent danger. *Hide!*

With his back to the monster, Blaze twisted and stumbled as he stared into the beast's black eyes. He yelped, pulling himself up against the wall. He limped and wailed in pain as he attempted to stand on his damaged foot. The beast growled with fierce aggression.

I must help him, she thought. Syra collected a stone from the alcove floor and hurled it beyond Blaze.

With an echoing thud, the stone severed the creature's attention, sending it charging along the pathway to inspect the noise.

Syra exhaled a sigh of relief, but before she could

emerge from the alcove to Blaze's aid, galloping footsteps stomped along a connecting tunnel, growing louder.

A hairless beast with fangs and claws, standing seven feet tall, dashed into the corridor. Bone-like spikes protruded from the creature's muscular shoulders, and the bones of its spine were like a bulging mountain range.

The monster curled its clawed fingers and gnashed its sharp fangs, and its foggy breath wafted about its pale face. The beast switched its head, locking its fiery gaze on the broken young man who dared to lurk in its abode.

Blaze staggered and dragged himself along the wall, away from Syra's position. He waved his light beam at its face.

"Syra . . . don't move. I'll draw it away." Blaze unfolded a pocket knife and thrust its tip at the monster.

Her axe beeped twice, and the sound trailed into the tunnel.

The beast whipped its head in her direction, grunting and growling, but she had wedged herself inside the cavity, hiding from its sight. Her hands and legs shook so forcefully that it felt like she was collapsing into paralysis.

Blaze shouted and stabbed his blade forward. "Get back, whatever you are." He hobbled along the path flashing his light in its eyes.

With ferocious strides, the bipedal monster slammed into Blaze, ploughing half his body through an opening in the wall. Syra heard the crunch of bone as the air was crushed from his lungs. His lamp tumbled onto the floor.

She saw his squashed head and his trembling arms dangling from the opening. Blood seeped from his mouth as he tried to speak. His eye sockets bulged as if he had been bashed in the face.

Syra covered her mouth in disgust. His limp body sent a

charge of adrenalin through her veins. Her hands continued to shake, and her heart pounded. She struggled to breathe in her attempt to be silent.

With a final jolt, Blaze's body was crunched and dragged through the edges of the gap.

Her light faulted, flickering on and off. In the pulsing light and the wafting dust, she watched more monsters charge across the tunnel, diving through the crevice beneath the wall.

She rested her head against the marble lining of the niche. Without warning, her lamp light flicked off. She could hear the knocking and popping sounds of their communication. A flurry of feet trampled the ground. She squeezed her eyes shut.

Leaning against the cold wall, she listened. The more she heard, the less animal-like they seemed to be.

The grunting sounds being exchanged followed staccato patterns. *They're talking to each other.*

Amid the strange sounds, Syra heard a distant whisper. Or at least she thought she did. The voice was not like the harsh communications she had just heard. Nor did the voice seem evil.

There was a commotion at the end of the corridor. She could hear the vile shrieks of the monsters. Sounds of flurrying thuds and whacks of attack echoed along the path, and a low boom shuddered the ground beneath her feet like the aftershocks of a bomb. *What is that? Do the monsters attack themselves? Are Tion and Kardia alive and fighting?*

Syra tried to quiet her mind and focused on the sonics. She released the clenching grip on her axe and lowered herself until she sat inside the marble recess.

Before long, the noises faded. Faint echoes resonated beyond the passageway walls. She inhaled and exhaled a controlled breath, and in the silence, she heard light feet padding across the floor. She flinched, bringing her knees to her chest. Whatever it was, it moved with slow, gentle steps.

Her heart vaulted into her throat. She tensed every muscle in her body. Then the steady padding of controlled footsteps approached her, and Syra crept up to her feet. The Kynorian axe pulsed, but the light was a soft blue. *The handle isn't vibrating. No monsters?*

She heard breathing. Human-like breathing.

"Syra . . . is that you?" a familiar voice asked.

Syra released a deep sigh. The voice was unmistakable. The ache in the pit of her stomach vanished. The back of her head felt healed. Warmth returned to her extremities, and hope and love overcame her heart. Syra shook her lamp, and it strobed back onto full light.

Her light revealed the greatest surprise.

"Telora!" She rushed forward and hugged her sister. "I thought you were gone for good. You're never leaving me ever again."

She pushed her nose into Telora's hair. A faint remnant of her perfume still lingered, laced with a strong scent of melaleuca. Syra kissed her forehead, and they embraced.

"Are you hurt?" Syra stepped away, analysing Telora to see if she was injured. "How did you survive down here? Are the other students alive?"

"The last forty-eight hours have been unimaginable," Telora said. "I'm the only one out of the group alive." She lowered her eyes, and her smile sank into a cold frown.

Syra forced her smile and pondered the unspeakable events her sister had experienced. She noticed Telora was draped in a thick, dark-blue cloak, pinned with a shining brooch carved with geometric patterns the likes of which

Syra had never seen. A grey, fleecy scarf covered her neck, and she wore black leather gloves on her hands.

"Telora, you don't seem like you've been stranded below the surface in a struggle for your life. You look refreshed and in good spirits." *Something isn't adding up.*

Telora nodded.

"Why are you dressed in that cloak?" Syra enquired as she rubbed the material of Telora's cloak between her fingers.

"The Kynorians," Telora said excitedly. "They're here. They gave me food, water, and this sweet floral elixir, which has given me strength. They've taken good care of me down here. Even though I've seen *things* I shouldn't have, I've felt quite safe around them."

"Kynorians are still living down here?" Syra asked.

"No, they're a reconnaissance team," Telora told her. "They were sent to scout the mines. One's a female named Etháni, the other is a male named Halekar. They're from the sacred island of Starfall, wherever that is, and they're majestic and kind. When they speak, it feels as if you're in a trance-like state. It's so soothing to hear them. Etháni is tall, stunning, and kind but intense at the same time. The rifas scream and cower at the sight of the imposing Halekar." Her eyes glinted, and her face brightened at their mention.

Etháni. Halekar. Syra imagined them like the majestic statues she saw in the earlier chamber.

"They are strange names." She could not believe Telora's luck.

"If it wasn't for them, I'd be dead."

Syra squinted at Telora. "Why didn't they help you out of this awful place?"

Telora aimed her light into the passageway. "We've been trapped on this level for an entire day and a half. They've been tracking some type of superbeast with supernatural powers. There are too many scary things that dwell down here, so it hasn't been easy for us to leave just yet." She panned her light along the opposite side of the corridor. "Etháni also told me they needed to locate an item of 'immense importance' before we could exit the mines, but they never said what it is."

Syra stared into the gloomy corridor, wondering what ancient mysteries might be hidden inside the forsaken Dura Mines.

"What could be so important," Syra said, "to lead them into an underworld filled with flesh-eating monsters?"

"I'm not exactly sure of their main purpose," Telora replied, "because when they talk together, it's in their Kynorian language. I've had no idea what they've been discussing, but I can sense a desperation in their words. Though they can speak our language with a heavy accent, they've said very little to me."

Syra smiled. "You smell like a larn tree."

"I know." Telora giggled. "Etháni dabbed melaleuca oil on my neck and underarms. They hate the smell of melaleuca."

"The monsters, you mean?" Syra was confused, hearing her words.

"The Kynorians call them *rifas*," Telora said. "*The Horde of the Underworld,* and the word rifa translates as 'abundant menace' in their language."

"Rifas," Syra whispered to herself.

Telora shook her head. "Something bad is about to happen. Not just in the mines. The Kynorians are deeply disturbed and say an ancient evil has returned to Númaria."

"Could it be the Denkarians?" Syra asked.

"Not exactly," Telora said. "They've given me an important letter to hand to 'our leader', whoever that is. She removed a folded piece of paper from her jacket. The waxy seal was green and gold. "Maybe you could give it to Edin, leader of the Firekites. He can be trusted." She handed the letter to Syra.

Syra slipped the letter inside her backpack. Before she could speak another word, a loud thump shuddered through the passageway, sending a tremor beneath their feet. Bellowing screeches issued along the southern tunnels.

Syra's head became heavy once again. Her vision blurred. Her heart strained to push the mainlined adrenalin swishing through her veins.

A glowing aura of orange and blue light spilled into the end of the corridor. Two mysterious voices called to Telora from behind the light, but apart from her name, the rest of their words were in a different language. Syra could barely make out the tall silhouettes at the end of the tunnel. Then they spoke words she could understand.

CHAPTER 10

A STRUGGLE TO THE SURFACE

A BURST of bright orange energy sizzled through the corridor, flashing the interior with its light.

A commanding masculine voice yelled at the end of the passage. "Keep to the wall, and do not move!"

Telora shoved Syra toward the wall, and they huddled behind a stone baluster.

A second burst of plasma flashed against the pillar, and a convulsing growl ascended. A third shot fired like a searing laser. Peering into her beam of light, Syra could see a rifa dragging its own crushed body toward the wall. A trail of blood pooled in its tracks. She covered her mouth. Her hands and feet tensed at the gory sight.

Syra held Telora's hand. "I'm not letting go of you until we're out of these mines."

The corridor fell to silence, and they ambled along the path toward the origin of the voice with their lights aimed into the looming passageway.

Syra noticed a warm glow emanating from an adjoining path sixty metres ahead. She watched as one of the tall figures she had seen earlier emerged from the light.

The edges of his cloak fluttered with his deep, long strides. His footsteps knocked upon the hard surface. He moved his hood aside and revealed shoulder-length smooth, black hair, woven with a swirling lace braid on one side of his head. His contoured face was pale yet radiated with sovereign power, and his sharp grey eyes gleamed, not like jewels but more like the argent moon on a crisp night.

Syra slowed and halted, with mouth agape in wonder.

Telora squeezed Syra's hand. "That's Halekar," she whispered.

"*Mar sienin erano,*" Halekar greeted Telora and bowed.

Telora bowed at Halekar, smiled, and faced Syra. "It means, *'May serenity be upon you'* in their language." She tilted her head to Halekar. "Is that right?"

His eyes stared into Syra's soul. "Indeed, your memory serves you well, Telora."

Syra gazed up at him with widened eyes. She felt as if he was contacting her telepathically. Her brow creased and then slowly released as her discomfort transformed into a serene feeling of stillness she had not felt in years.

Towering at six feet, six inches, he was the tallest and most kingly individual she had ever seen. A sheathed sword with a blue jewel on its pommel was strapped to his back.

Slung atop his shoulder was a black, contoured rifle, unlike the Denkarian soldiers' short cylindrical rifles. Its thick barrel was covered in hexagonal patterns. The rifle's trigger guard was wide enough to conceal a hand, and the transparent chamber was filled with an orange liquid. *It's what made the bright orange flash.*

Halekar peered into Syra's eyes as if he understood her thoughts. "My weapon is an Isoburst multi-mode plasma generator."

Syra stepped away, astonished by his statement. In the

corner of her vision, she saw another glowing light spring from the same adjoining path Halekar came from.

Marching into the passage was a female Kynorian.

This must be Etháni, Syra thought as she gazed upon her in awe.

Her face beamed with a luminance Syra had not seen before. Her light footsteps could barely be heard along the corridor. She lowered her Isoburst rifle and, moving her cloak to the side, fastened her rifle to her waist. A blade was strapped to her upper thigh. Her long, black hair was woven into a descending ladder braid, dangling upon her left shoulder. A slender, transparent alloy crown with a bright green jewel mantled her head.

Syra gazed upon her and noticed her symmetrical face seemed grim yet glimmered with stunning elegance and finesse, unlike the mortal women she knew. Syra could not lower her gaze from Etháni's bright turquoise eyes, which were not like jewels but more like the currents glistening in the shallow rock pools of the west coast. Across her back was strapped a dark axe.

Etháni's physical height was great by mortal standards, and the tip of her head met Halekar's nose.

They whispered in their Kynorian tongue while Telora and Syra waited in silence.

Etháni faced Syra. "Your eyes are glazed." She inspected her face. "Your skin is dry. You must hydrate." She handed Syra a squeeze pouch filled with water.

Syra guzzled the cool water, pouring it down her throat, savouring each drop as if it was her last. She handed the empty pouch to Etháni.

Halekar removed a vial from his cloak and slipped it into Syra's grasp. "This is *Viata*," he said, "an elixir from my land of Starfall. Sip only a mouthful of the liquid, and you shall feel revived."

Syra inspected the teardrop-shaped glass vial, enclosed in a geometric webbing made from a platinum-like alloy. Before drinking the potion, she glanced at Telora, who smiled and nodded. Syra removed the lid and lifted the vial to her lips.

A syrupy-sweet scent of spices and blossoms entered her nose and mouth. She felt her nostrils expand and her lungs open as she inhaled the fragrance.

She drizzled the liquid onto her tongue and swallowed. Closing her eyes, she breathed controlled breaths, and her heart rate slowed. The stinging pain in her head subsided, and she slowly opened her eyes. Her strained vision had improved, and she felt revitalised.

"I feel as if I've slept for hours." Syra straightened her posture and smiled at the joy of the elixir's magical properties.

"One mouthful shall fortify you for days," Etháni said. "Your strength is needed, especially for what shall happen in this pit." She glanced at Halekar.

Syra felt her stomach sink at Etháni's words.

A squawking shriek resonated at the end of the passage, and a clanking noise echoed on the opposite side.

Halekar spun around and lifted the Isoburst to his eye. A holographic scope appeared above the chamber. Red dots multiplied in the scope's display, causing Halekar to step away.

Etháni dropped to her knee and placed her flat palm against the floor. She closed her eyes and whispered to herself.

The warrioress opened her eyes and rose. "*Atroi eínate ero, Halekar*," she said swiftly.

Syra hugged Telora into a clinch and felt her sister's hands quivering.

"What's wrong?" Syra asked Etháni. "What are you saying?"

Rapid sounds of clicking and popping bounced along the passage, followed by the clanging of steel against stone.

"We are being hunted," Etháni responded.

Halekar lowered his weapon and stared at Syra with his piercing eyes. "Can you hear it?" He motioned to the end of the corridor. "The noises the rifas make, it is called echolocating. These malign creatures survey and navigate the underworld with this primal mechanism. Their physical forms are many, though I do not wish to elucidate them here while we remain within their abode."

A rumbling tremor bellowed through the Dura Mines, shaking the floor beneath their feet. Syra and Telora stumbled in an attempt to stabilise themselves. Halekar and Etháni stood like monumental effigies of might with their weapons forward.

Sand and debris drizzled through the Kynorian's panning lights shining into the passage. Hooting and growling rifas dashed across the path, only to disappear into the adjoining lanes.

Etháni fired multiple bursts of plasma.

Packs of rifas poured from ramps and lanes on either side into the corridor. They bobbed their blood-smeared faces and swung their clawed hands. The harsh screeches and the slapping of their feet upon the floor sent shivers along Syra's spine.

"There must be hundreds of them," Syra shouted, staring at the massing rifas creeping forward and biting the air.

Telora gasped and squeezed Syra's hand, her young sister's vision trapped in the horde's haunting gaze.

Etháni retrieved a palm-sized sphere from inside her cloak. She removed the pin from the globe and launched it at the rifas. With blazing yellow light, the grenade exploded on impact before the rifas, swirling a cyclonic inferno around them. As their bodies burned, the beasts squealed and dispersed, scattering into crevices and lanes.

Syra and Telora shielded their eyes from the scorching flames twenty metres away. Syra felt its heat on her face and hands as smoke wafted to the corridor's ceiling. She had witnessed Denkarian bombs explode, but the blazing firestorm the Kynorian grenade created was far more advanced.

Halekar ushered Syra and Telora through a tall archway into a long, winding staircase.

Etháni tarried and fired more shots into the rifas. Still, their numbers multiplied, and their raging cries rang throughout the underworld.

Inside the damp, ascending staircase, Syra saw lamps mounted high up on the curved brick walls. She held Telora's hand as she chased Halekar, trying desperately to keep up with him. Her lungs felt like they were burning. *I don't know how much longer I can take it.*

Syra heard Etháni's heated voice resonate up into the staircase from below.

"*Taras Antra!*" Etháni yelled with fury.

Syra felt the walls and steps tremble, not like a thunderous ground-shuddering quake but more like the stomping of giant feet.

Halekar came to a halt, slowing Syra and Telora with his hand. He crept to the far wall and peered down the stairs.

"What now? Syra asked, her panting breaths echoing along the stairs.

He wrenched his body. "*Taras Antra*," he answered, "a cave troll."

Telora yanked Syra's hand. "I've seen the cave trolls before. They're giant monsters strong enough to pick you up and snap your arms off."

"Cave trolls are real?" Syra could not reconcile the plausibility of these giants existing. "I thought they were stories, folklore."

Telora gazed into her eyes and quickly shook her head. "They're very real."

Syra felt the dampening sweat upon her brow. She tilted her head to Halekar, whose body cast great shadows against the lamplight.

"*Ethánia*," he shouted. "*Posa ese ekeri?*" How many are there?

"*Déteri*," she called. Two.

A fist-sized rock came tumbling from the apex of the staircase, causing Telora and Syra to flinch. A racket of barking and stabbing shrieks descended from above.

Syra flicked her light up the stairs but saw nothing but the dusty steps and the damp walls.

The shaky light of Eth
áni's Isoburst reflected off the walls as she vaulted up the steps.

The stone staircase shuddered with the stomping staccato of percussive thumping. Low, chomping growls resonated below like the crashing waves of the sea.

Ethání arrived at the midway point of the stairs with her weapon drawn. "The cave trolls are here," she uttered. "The basement level is now compromised."

"The north drain is our only exit," Halekar said. "It shall be less guarded in their absence."

"What if we cannot reach it in time," Ethâni remarked as she glanced at Syra and Telora. "Drawing out the cave trolls has consequences."

The walls vibrated in convulsing waves, and crushed rocks fell from the fractured cornices.

"Ready your Kynorian axe," Halekar told Syra, pointing to the glowing weapon. "It may serve you well. Follow me."

Syra slid the axe from the strap and gripped the handle forcefully.

Ethâni's warm hand caressed Syra's face. Her eyes sparkled like the stars in the Hydroverse. "Aim for the neck and chest. Find your courage and shine like the light of your great mortal ancestors. The perils begin now."

Through Ethâni's touch, Syra felt a mystical energy transfer into her body. She inched backward and stared at the warrioress contemplating who her mortal ancestors were. Her mind flashed multiple visions of their triumphant exfiltration from the Dura Mines. She envisioned the sun on her face and the winds streaming through the trees. With Telora by her side and the sanctuary of the Kynorian's presence, hope ascended inside her heart.

Halekar leaped up the steps with speed and agility.

Telora nudged Syra into motion, and they sped after him with Ethâni trailing behind them.

The stairs wound twice before straightening. The foundations trembled as the roaring cave trolls hammered up the staircase.

Ethâni's voice projected from above Syra's head. "*Ese montar, Halekar. Ese aronti!*" *They are close. They are coming.*

The guttural tones of the cave trolls were so loud it felt like they were only a few metres away from Syra, and goosebumps triggered along her spine and arms.

Breathing the stale underground air, Syra struggled to

keep up with Halekar. She glanced across her shoulder and was relieved to see Telora leaping upon each step behind her.

Halekar slowed his pace on reaching the zenith of the staircase. Syra halted with Telora at her side. She stared at the Kynorian as he crept forward onto the landing, his weapon drawn, his shoulders taut.

CHAPTER 11
PERILOUS PATHS

PUFFED AND WHEEZING FOR AIR, Syra slowly climbed up to the landing. Their path opened into a vast gallery with carbon steel buttresses conjoining pillars against glass-like walls. Overgrown ferns had sprouted from the mezzanine floor above, rising to the second tier of seating. Strangling vines and creeping mosses draped the elegant Kynorian statues flanking the causeway through the gallery's centre.

Five tall archways adjoined the gallery on each side, and water dripped from a glass sphere suspended fifty metres above them.

To Syra's surprise, she saw glass panels on the ceiling covered in foliage, and thin beams of natural light streamed through them. She sighed. "I never thought I'd be so happy seeing the sunlight."

"It's beautiful," Telora added, gazing up.

Etháni climbed the last few steps below and aimed her Isoburst down the stairwell.

A darting arrow swished past Syra's face, flicking her hair. More arrows flew from the edges of the gallery, barely missing them. She turned to face Telora and felt her feet lift from the floor. Halekar carried her and Telora, placing them behind a broad pillar to the side of the opening.

Barbaric, human-like voices hollered at the end of the gallery. She saw sturdy, bearded wildmen, mantled in furs and armed with bows and spiked bludgeons. They charged at them like frenetic savages.

The stairwell reverberated with a grating roar. Syra spun around and clutched Telora.

The cave trolls smashed the walls, and their vile gaze branded Syra's soul.

Etháni flipped a switch on her Isoburst, and an orb of orange light swelled about the rifle's chamber. With a boom and flash, a burst of plasma fired from the muzzle, singeing the shoulder of the first monster. The troll stumbled and growled, clasping the wound on its shoulder.

The second cave troll stomped up the steps, bashing its way through. Its ears had been cut off, and a flat, scared nose poked from its face. The troll's body was covered in spiked armour, and the beast wielded a massive square-faced hammer.

Etháni leaped upon the landing and fired at the buttress of the stairwell ceiling. Cracked stones crumbled and crashed upon the cave trolls. The gallery's archway fractured in the wake of her shot.

A phalanx of fifty barbarians unleashed another volley of arrows at Halekar. In the Kynorian's hand lay an alloy rod. A bright blue light enveloped his palm and forearm. With a commanding cry, he punched his fist forward. A wave of strident energy fractured the arrows, truncating their trajectory. The first echelon of wildmen was flung backward as the men tumbled upon the floor.

Buried beneath the rubble, one of the surviving cave

trolls jolted and pummelled its way out, flinging rocks and dust about the stairwell.

Peering ahead, Syra saw the squared drain exit Ethání had mentioned on the lower section of the wall at the end of the gallery. Sunlight streamed from its edges. "The way out!" she shouted, jutting her finger at it.

A rising wave of rifa screeches filled the gallery.

Beasts scuttled to their foul chieftains from adjoining paths until the entire causeway was filled. Their foaming mouths raged, and their ropey bodies weaved through the statues like scrabbling scorpions.

She felt the air siphoning from her lungs at the shock of the rifas' numbers.

Halekar launched a grenade into the causeway. The bomb exploded on the marble floor, flash-freezing multiple beasts inside its fifteen-metre blast radius. He fired his Isoburst at the frosted rifas, and their bodies shattered like broken glass.

Syra stood in front of Telora and double-gripped her axe. She heard the smashing of stones behind her. As she turned, she saw the cave troll swing its hammer at Ethání.

The Kynorian warrioress slid across the floor and dropped beneath the flying hammer. The strike pulverised the wall with a clonk, burying the hammer beneath the crumbled ruins. The troll ripped and kicked at the stuck weapon and attempted to yank it from the rubble.

Ethání unsheathed her axe and leaped upon the giant's shoulders. With a spearing swing, she stabbed the axe blade through the cave troll's head. Its thick limbs fibrillated, and black blood streamed down its dirty face and chest as it choked.

Ethání heaved the embedded axe blade from the beast's skull with a soaring scream, flinging its blood upon the floor. The troll yelped as the sizzling axe blade was ripped from its body.

Syra's mouth was agape, watching as Etháni descended the cave troll, landing steadily on her feet. The monster's black eyes flickered, and its dead body slammed upon the steps.

The bursts of plasma from Halekar's weapon boomed and thumped. The more rifas he killed, the faster their ranks replenished in what seemed an immortal supply of malevolence.

Halekar's Isoburst beeped and powered off. He sighed and lowered the rifle from his firing stance.

"What happened?" Syra asked.

He flipped a switch and waved his hand across the weapon's plasma chamber. "Isoburst rifles have a cool-down period after overheating."

"How long is the cool-down period?" Syra stared at the orange plasma slowly refilling the chamber.

"Roughly fifteen seconds," he told her.

A lone rifa with a hide mask and a sharpened shank in its grasp screeched and leaped at Halekar from the gallery floor.

Syra raised her axe, sidestepped, and swung the blade into the rifa's chest. The creature convulsed upon the floor, dragging its freezing body toward the Kynorian.

Halekar unsheathed his blade and thrust its tip into the beast's neck, killing it. He turned and stared at Syra with his piercing eyes and bowed.

Syra smiled and gave him an awkward nod. She glanced at the frosty steam issuing from the axe's blue, glowing blade.

From atop the upper mezzanine of the gallery, rifas plunged until thousands of them swarmed the ground floor.

The ten remaining barbarians charged through the rifas, killing the beasts with their crude weapons as they stomped toward the company.

Syra's axe vibrated with the presence of the oncoming rifas. She stepped behind Halekar as her hands quivered.

Telora peered inside the gallery. "If we can't reach the exit, where do we go, Etháni?"

The warrioress panned her light about the landing, scanning the corners and ceiling. Her light reflected off a silver ledge three metres above the eastern wall.

Above the ledge, Syra saw a wide opening. Not a crudely carved hole with wafting fumes and dripping water. The entrance was more like an observation balcony.

Etháni sheathed her axe and scaled the eastern wall. She lifted herself to the ledge and disappeared.

Syra marched to the wall and shook her head at Etháni vanishing. "Where did she go?"

Telora aimed her light up at the opening. "I don't know."

Halekar's Isoburst beeped, signalling its replenishment. "Cover yourselves!" He launched another grenade into the rifas.

He leaped behind the pillar. A windstorm of fire roared, burning the edges of the gallery entrance.

The Kynorian flames were so hot Syra felt their heat across her hands and face. Telora winced and hugged Syra into a clinch.

The cauterised rifas wailed in agony, but beyond their shrieks came a war cry of damned voices.

"Their numbers increase!" Halekar shielded his face from the raging flames. Leaping to the side, he shot the archway keystone. Slabs of rock hurtled down, blocking the entrance. He stared at Syra. "Where is Etháni?"

"She left us, Halekar," Syra screamed. "Why would she leave now?"

The Kynorian gave Syra a taut smile. "We would never leave you down here."

Listening to Halekar's final words, Syra saw a glowing light from the opening above. The light brightened until Etháni's face emerged from the threshold.

"Halekar," Etháni called, "we face yet another problem."

Lifting his gaze to hers, Halekar's smile inverted. "Is there an exit?" His gloves squeaked as he gripped his Isoburst.

"Indeed, there is," Etháni answered, "though the path will bring us upon . . ." She paused and quickly glanced at Syra before returning her eyes to Halekar. "*Eno buranith tolia.*"

"What are you saying?" Syra demanded. "By the worried look in your eyes, you don't seem confident."

"We must pass a rifa nest," Halekar told Syra.

Etháni fixed her stare at Syra. "The rifas are in their primary feeding cycle. Guided by the phases of the moon, they are most dangerous and aware during their feeding."

Syra clutched onto Telora. She felt her mind reeling, and the terror of the rifas feeding brought a flood of anxiety that washed into the rest of her body. *What are they feeding on?* Syra feared. *Will we make it out of this pit?*

Etháni outreached her hand. "We must hurry, our window of time draws to its end, and the path ahead is fraught with hazard."

The gallery archway shuddered, and rifas clawed at the blocked entry, scratching and shrieking with primeval bloodlust. More beasts climbed the stairwell from below, barking and snarling as they vaulted the cracked steps.

Before Syra could speak a word, she felt the broad hands

of Halekar lift her upon the wall. She smelled citrus and sweet spices on his skin.

She caught Etháni's hand and climbed up the ledge.

Halekar hauled Telora onto his back and scaled the wall, evading the massing rifas below.

"Switch your lamps off," Etháni said to Syra and Telora. "Keep between Halekar and me and remain silent."

Syra swallowed. "Will we ever get out of here?" Her hands shook as she switched her lamp off.

Halekar held his finger to his lips and peered into Syra's eyes but gave her no answer.

Syra watched Etháni adjust the light on her Isoburst to a soft amber glow as she crept forward like a stealthy panthera.

Halekar silently ushered Syra and Telora in single file after Etháni, taking his place at rear guard.

Syra ambled along the narrow access tunnel. Its ceiling was low enough to force the Kynorians to hunch as they moved. The walls inside the passage were furrowed with machined grooves, and a titanium upper ledge held the cylindrical lamps of the ancient lighting system.

She felt Telora's cold hand slip inside hers, and she glanced behind. *How did we end up down here?* She aimed her weary gaze forward at Etháni, who traversed the inclining tunnel with light feet. *Why is this happening to us?*

The passage wound and dipped into a long, narrow corridor with pipes, ten inches in diameter, lining the ceiling. Vapours steamed from the pipes, and the condensation dripped upon the walls.

Syra heard their footsteps and the controlled breathing of Halekar behind her.

After trekking ninety metres with nothing but Etháni's low light to guide them, the corridor wound left. A biting stench filled Syra's nostrils and mouth, and she winced in its omnipotent presence.

Ethání slowed her pace and held them back with her outreached hand. Ethání motioned Halekar ahead, and the Kynorian brushed past Syra with his holographic scope raised to his eyes.

Syra released Telora's hand and clasped the handle of her axe, and it began to vibrate inside her grip, glowing with soft, orange light. She stared at Telora, whose eyes widened at the sight of the axe's light.

Ethání gently gathered the girls to the nearby wall. Syra saw steadfast gaze. Her heart thumped and a sharp stitch developed above her diaphragm.

She peered into the corridor and watched Halekar inch toward what she could define as a recess along the wall. Taking his last step, he halted and raised his hand. With two slow hand motions, he waved them to his position.

Ethání placed Telora's hands upon Syra's waistband and escorted them to Halekar.

The air had become stifling, and Syra felt the putrid reek of rotting flesh and faeces permeating her body. As they reached Halekar, she thought she could hear what sounded like the quick panting of multiple people ahead.

Halekar held the Isoburst in his right hand and quietly unsheathed his sword with his left. Its blade pulsed with soft, blue light, but the light began to infuse with black and red veins.

An archway appeared along the left wall. He slowly aimed the rifle's amber light into the opening.

Syra stared inside and froze, fearing Halekar's light would startle the rifas, but the beasts did not seem to detect his amber light.

He illuminated the tops of rifa heads as they bobbed. A

squelching pain grew within Syra's stomach, not solely from the stench but from the one hundred-odd rifas crammed inside a room and the danger of stirring them.

On swift feet, Halekar and Etháni quietly led the girls along the passage away from the rifa-filled room.

Ascending a short staircase to an upper level, they approached the opening of another room. Halekar aimed his light above and revealed twenty eviscerated corpses hanging upside down from the ceiling, fastened by the ankles with rusted chains.

Squinting in the low amber light, Syra caught a glimpse of the circular Grandinem emblem upon the blood-soaked jacket of one corpse. She felt Telora's knuckles tremble against her lower back. Syra covered her mouth. Her pulse throbbed from her chest into her neck, and her forehead dampened in the presence of the rising heat. She turned her head away and kept her eyes on Halekar.

A whacking noise echoed into the passage thirty metres ahead. The Kynorians ushered them farther along the corridor, passing three steel doors and a hallway leading to a staircase blocked with spikes and wires.

Halekar slowly turned to face them. His eyes beamed at Etháni, who held guard at the rear.

He tilted his head toward the dark room they were about to approach.

Aiming his light into the room's edges, he revealed fifty rifas gathered about a steel bench. Water dripped upon the bench from cracks in the ceiling above, and steam hissed from a fractured wall vent in the corner of the room.

A towering rifa stood before the bench casting a colossal shadow against the wall. In the fiend's grasp was a crude cleaver with a crimson handle, but this rifa did not resemble any of the other rifas. It had long plumes of thick matted hair. Its body was tall and muscular, unlike the sinewy, ropey bodies of the scavenger rifas.

The monster's shoulders rose and fell like tidal waves as it inhaled and exhaled deep, husky breaths.

Halekar slowly tilted his Isoburst, and its light illuminated the lifeless body of a blonde woman tied to the dripping bench.

CHAPTER 12
THE PIT OF THE SCAVENGERS

SYRA SQUINTED as she struggled to see the sullied face of the woman in the faint glow. She traced her sight along the woman's arm and saw a bandaged wrist covered in blood.

Kardia . . . Syra inhaled a quick breath. Her entire body tensed like a crumpled clump of steel wool.

The hybrid beast clamped onto Kardia's bruised wrist, extending her arm upon the bench. It raised its filthy hand. The blade glinted in the reflecting light. With a belting swing, the monster severed her arm at the shoulder. The strike reverberated through the room and into the corridor.

Syra squeezed her eyes shut. Images of Tion and Kardia splintered her mind, and she recalled the gentle tone of Kardia's voice inside her head. A voice that had been slain in the gelid, forbidding underworld of the Dura Mines.

A pack of skulking rifas with burned faces crept into the room from a connecting hallway on the opposite side. Aiming their noses to the ceiling, they sniffed the air like ravenous thylacines. The stench of charred flesh and faeces infused the room with sickness. Clicking and popping, the vile creatures scanned the floor and walls panning their gaze toward the archway.

Halekar inched backward silently and lowered his light. He stared at Ethāni, motioning her attention toward the end of the corridor. With a slow sweeping motion, he aimed his light at the centre of the room.

The hybrid beast swung its cleaver repeatedly, hacking Kardia's limbs.

Syra flinched with every strike, only to be comforted by the firm squeeze of Telora's hand.

The vile butcher flung the severed limbs to the scavenger rifas like a murderous servant of the damned.

The monsters squawked and growled as they chomped and gnawed the flesh, cracking through bone and tearing through sinew.

Syra's chest quivered so quickly she could not breathe. In her darkened mind, she saw no end to the horror.

Halekar waved them on, and they crept to the end of the corridor. The Kynorian aimed his Isoburst's light into the east bend, scanning the path.

Syra smelt the burning reek of ash and fire, and the charred scent lingered in her throat.

Twenty metres along the passage rose two pillars, each one four metres in height. The marble pillars were carved with vertical Národan runes, and a golden insignia of the axe and the hammer sat at each pillar's zenith.

Halekar gathered them behind the left pillar and fixed his commanding stare on Ethāni. As far as Syra could see, the Kynorians appeared to be communicating telepathically. It could have simply been their understanding of the underworld and all its evils.

Ethāni rested her hand on Telora's shoulder, and once again, she raised her finger to her lips and shook her head.

Etháni nodded to Halekar, and their lights simultaneously switched off.

Syra seized Telora, resting her head against her sister's cheek as the blackness trawled through her soul.

Etháni reached for Syra and clasped her cold, tremoring hand. She felt warmth and comfort transferring into her heart as if Etháni could feel her anguish and fear. The Kynorian released Syra's hand, and the silken glow of her rifle's hologram cast a soft light upon her face.

The hologram displayed a three-dimensional render of the hall's interior. She panned her weapon from left to right.

Halekar had positioned himself behind the opposite pillar, staring into his scope.

As Etháni swept through the hall, Syra noticed the random red dots within her scope.

With a wave of Etháni's fingers, a light from her weapon ignited the hall's interior with a reddish hue. The light was more of a darkness replacement, a kind of night-vision enhancement that converted the darkness to light.

Syra saw a long vast hall roughly eighty metres in length. Tall stone tables on the left wall were placed every three metres. Along the right wall, the rubble of cracked statues of Kynorian kings and queens lay scattered about the floor. The remains of blackened bones and piled bonfires appeared randomly through the hall's centre. A stench of putrefying corpses wafted from the entrance.

Sweeping her rifle to the left, Etháni paused. She slowly inched her eyes away from the scope and faced Halekar.

Lowering his Isoburst, Halekar glanced at Etháni and gave her a nod.

Syra crept forward to get a closer look into the hall. She took a quick breath and stared at the scattered rifas standing with their heads bowed and shoulders hunched. She heard their rasping breaths.

These monsters were tall and mangled. Their transfigured bodies were covered in giant boils, and the skin on their shoulders and arms looked like the striations of a dried riverbed. A musty smell lingered about the entrance, the kind of decaying scent of moulding flesh.

On the tips of her toes, Syra whispered into Etháni's ear. "What are they?"

Etháni lowered her Isoburst and faced Syra and Telora. "Infected rifas," she whispered, pointing into the hall. "We call them *Sleeping Willows*. They rest, semi-dormant. We must walk past them. If you crouch and move slowly, they should not notice you."

Syra peered into the blackness of the hall. She saw few details from a distance, but random burbling noises rumbled from the hunched beasts. Their gnarled bodies momentarily jittered in their temporary stasis.

"Stay behind Halekar," Etháni whispered. "I shall cover from the rear. Breathe through your nose when inside the hall, for these rifas can detect the bio-chemistry inside your mouth."

"What if they wake up?" Syra quavered.

"Pray it does not happen," Etháni said. "For your own sake, do not gaze upon their faces."

Syra felt the vision of the warrioress reach inside her core. A shiver ran from her spine into her ears.

Halekar twisted and motioned Etháni inside the hall.

With his weapon raised, he crept across the threshold. Etháni guided the girls behind him, and they crouched and trod stealthily.

Syra inhaled the mouldy, warm air of the hall through her nose. Creaking noises from dark corners reverberated, causing her to flinch. Her axe vibrated heavily as she squeezed its grip, a warning of her proximity to the rifas. Her heart laboured inside her chest, and her leg muscles strained with each crouching movement.

Guided by Halekar's dim light, Syra traced his steps. Telora followed quietly behind her as they passed the first row of tables.

Torn clothing and mangled boots lay strewn about the floor. Dust, two inches thick, covered the broken chairs stacked in a four-metre-high pile. Fine debris particles glinted in Halekar's light.

The lumpy sounds of the rifas' staggered breathing circled her. Some of the monsters lay prostrate on the ground, and others rested on both knees.

At the centre, Halekar wove his way through the statues on bent knees before coming to a halt. He aimed his light to the left.

At the fringe of his light, Syra could barely see the torso of a towering rifa. Its shadow climbed high against the wall like a sharp mountain, claiming the underworld. She raised her gaze to the colossal rifa, standing with its head bowed. At its feet lay a spiked hammer with a recurved blade upon its apex. In the low light, she could barely see above its chest.

Lowering her stare to the beast's chest, she noticed worm-like tentacles squelching, reflecting in the light.

What are those squirming things? She thought.

She saw stitches upon the rifa's upper abdomen, not like those of a bound wound but more like clamped staples conjoining raw flesh.

She felt the touch of Ethani's hand, a reminder to keep her eyes lowered.

One by one, they passed the giant cryptic rifa as Halekar led them through the centre of the hall.

After thirty metres, he slowed, bringing them to a halt. His light revealed a clutter of ruined buttresses, cracked stone slabs, and other structural beams once used to prop and strengthen the hall's interior.

No. Syra stared at the blockage. *There better be a way through this mess.*

Bending his knees, Halekar illuminated a gap beneath two thick beams, which appeared to lead into the next section of the hall. From the floor, he turned and nodded to Etháni, and on his hands and knees, he disappeared inside the gap.

Syra slid her axe into the strap on her backpack and crawled in after him. Telora and Etháni followed her.

Syra moved beneath the beam, tracing Halekar's hand and knee prints. She crawled through the shell of a long steel cage before turning left and right.

Tilting her head to the left side, she froze and gripped the floor with numb fingers. A slapping sound emanated from no more than two metres away. She watched Etháni's light pass across two blood-covered rifas on their knees. The monsters flinched and knocked their heads on the floor as they wheezed and coughed.

A bead of sweat dripped upon Syra's nose, and she silently crawled to the end of the long table above her. Rising to her feet, she peered into the passage leading out of the hall. She saw dormant rifas scattered as far as Halekar's light extended.

Telora and Etháni emerged from beneath the table.

Halekar directed them along the passage, but scavengers filled every corner. The spaces between the beasts were littered with fallen pillars, thick rods of steel, and metre-high stacks of mortal skulls.

Halekar navigated right, stepping into a parallel corridor. As they passed into the next pathway, Halekar held them back.

Syra saw clumps of green, glowing palm-sized globules clustered upon the walls and floors and sprawling onto the high ceiling. Quadrupedal rifas with protruding rib cages and short tails coughed and choked. Their bodies fibrillated in the darkness.

Syra tasted the toxic, acidic air on her tongue. Fumes poured from the glowing clusters as if they were alive and breathing.

"What is that?" Syra whispered, tugging on Halekar's arm.

"Poisonous vapours," he whispered to her, "cover your mouths." He gestured to Syra and Telora.

Syra wrapped her mouth and nose with her scarf, and Telora lifted her shirt, covering her mouth and nose.

Strangely, the Kynorians did not cover their mouths. Instead, they withdrew small vials of yellow liquid and inhaled their vapours.

They crossed the threshold of a triangular archway draped in stringy cobwebs and arrived at a broad, L-shaped room. Halekar scanned the room's interior with his light.

Syra could see more of the quadruped rifas, but these beasts vomited a fetid, green ooze. She winced and tore her gaze from them.

The ruins of a marble pillar lay scattered across the floor, obstructing their path. Halekar lifted Syra and Telora over the column, and they advanced into the next section of the room.

A deep grunt thumped the air ahead of them, followed

by a low roar. Halekar summoned the girls behind a group of overturned tables.

The unexpected sound shot through Syra like a frequency of terror designed to freeze her soul.

In the Kynorian's light, she saw an immense rifa, more prominent than the others, ripping the flesh from its own shoulder and staggering about the room. With her cold stare, she froze, caught in the biting shock of her fears.

Her hopes of reaching the light slowly stripped away as she held her breath in dismay. Surrounded by rifas, she realised the imminent perils that lay before her. Even in the presence of the Kynorians, her mind squealed in fear.

CHAPTER 13
DARKNESS OF THE ABYSS

HALEKAR USHERED them through a doorway to the right side, leading into a parallel pathway littered with broken pipes. Cages, one metre in length, lined the left wall, and inside them were the glowing clusters they had seen in the previous hall. Black nets hung from the ceiling, and swirling rifa art, painted in blood, had been smeared upon the walls.

The path widened and lowered into a passage filled with snorting, wheezing rifas. Halekar motioned them into a side passage, clear except for a crumbled weapons rack leaning against the wall. The swords, maces, and axes were crudely fashioned with embedded spikes and rusted wires binding the handles.

The sound of splashing water echoed ahead. Halekar entered the winding passage, and his light revealed a ten-metre by ten-metre room. At the centre of the room, spitting water dripped from a crack in the ceiling that pooled on the floor.

At the far left corner of the room, four transformed, human-like rifas huddled over a bloodied corpse, tearing flesh from it. Their teeth snapped on bone, and their squelching tongues sucked the fatty pink marrow.

Ethàni's light scanned the corpse, and Syra clamped her mouth shut, taking trembling breaths through her nose. She saw the compass and the water canister dangling from the jacket of the young male. *Turtle.* She rubbed her eyes in the hope she was imagining a morbid nightmare.

One of the rifas flinched and cranked its neck in their direction. The beast gnawed at the dripping hunk of flesh in its mouth.

The Kynorians dimmed their lights to a pale luminance. They directed the girls behind the broken shelving along the wall and away from the feeding beasts.

They entered an empty corridor, forty metres in length, leading to a set of closed sliding doors. Dim glowing lights were fixed on the ceiling of the passage, spanning five metres apart.

Halekar arrived at the doors first, and Ethàni aimed her light through the two-inch gap between them. With a grunt, Halekar separated the sliding doors, forcing them apart with his hands.

With a cranking jolt, he opened them enough to reveal a chamber with a glass-panelled, domed ceiling. A detailed map of the mines glowed upon the far black wall.

A translucent titanium panel lay at the room's centre on a metre-high marble pedestal, and a radiant purple light illuminated its edges.

Thin beams of sunlight streamed from the cracked dome upon the centre of the room like ethereal spires from the heavens. Green and blue lights, two inches in diameter, faded in and out on the top corner of the left wall, and a thin ray of laser light from the panel connected them.

It's some type of tracking system, Syra thought.

As Halekar was about to step inside, a rifa with white eyes and an exoskeleton leaped into the corridor.

It stood seven feet tall. Its body was pale except for the plexus of purple veins sprawled across its chest and arms. Sharp blade-like bones projected from its shoulders. Its kinetic jaw separated, opening its mouth to a double row of serrated teeth. Its snake-like tongue was barbed, and reddish saliva dripped upon its chest.

The superbeast clung to the shadows, avoiding the light. Crawling on its hands and feet, it whipped its neck to the door and snarled.

Ethámi shoved Telora and Syra inside the room. Forcing them into a squat, she pushed them behind a steel container and knelt beside them.

Halekar leaped through the doors and crouched on the opposite side, aiming his Isoburst through the opening. He motioned them to remain still and silent.

The monster rose like an effigy of hatred. It lifted its gaze to the ceiling and unleashed a screeching cry. The bellow travelled along the corridor, funnelling into the parallel paths and nearby passages.

From the space between the doors, Syra could see the beast's shadow along the floor, drawing closer to them. With her back against the wall, she listened to the harsh rasping and clicking noises spilling through the gap. With heavy footsteps, the beast crept forward until the tip of its nose crossed the threshold of the doors.

The dim ceiling light revealed deep channels upon its broad nose and forehead. Slash marks surrounded its eye sockets like swirls of jagged bark on a tree trunk. The rifas' ghastly eyes were red with solid black pupils. Thick tusks protruded from its kinetic jaw.

Inching farther inside the opening, the rifa's mouth

expanded, and from it issued a decayed vapour, followed by a pulsing gurgle. The cruel vibrations of sound forced Syra's body to contract, sending shivers down her neck.

A distant metallic clang reverberated along the corridor and into the room.

The creature wrenched its neck and barked before withdrawing from the door opening. It vaulted backward, scrambling with hammering footsteps along the corridor and skidding left into a side passage.

"Quickly now," Halekar whispered. "Follow me." He hurried to a door at the end of the room.

They marched swiftly after him as he led them to a steel staircase dripping with water. A diffuse fog lay about the steps as they climbed to the second level of the main complex.

Upon the landing, Syra winced and began retching from the sour reek that filled her nose and mouth. She turned to Telora, who was smothering her nose and mouth.

Staring ahead at what appeared to be a foyer with many compartmentalised rooms, Syra saw half-eaten, mutilated mortal bodies lying in mangled formations about the floor. They wove between the marble benches with ancient saws and pickaxes upon them, and they followed Halekar onto a connecting hallway leading to a gallery.

Syra felt a moment of vertigo as she panned her gaze about the level. Piles of vent casings and chairs appeared scattered about the floor. A two-metre hole had been cut into the ceiling's centre and multiple archways led to unknown passages and stairwells. *This place is a maze*, she thought.

Before they arrived at the archway into the gallery, a fluttering growl reverberated above them.

Etháni and Halekar halted and switched their weapon

lights to a bright ultraviolet light beam. They scanned the hole in the ceiling. A rifa leaped over the hole, and

it disappeared, squawking into the above level.

Other shrill, croaking noises echoed beyond the foundations. Thumping footsteps stomped above them, circling their position.

Syra clutched onto Telora. She could feel her sister's quick breaths against her neck.

"I don't want to die here," Telora whispered, and a tear welled in her eye.

Telora's words galvanised Syra into action, and she clasped Etháni's arm. "Get us out of this place!"

Etháni peeled Syra's grip from her arm. "We draw near to the exit," she whispered. "The creature we just saw in the previous corridor is an *Aberrant,* a powerful rifa of the shadows, a darker evil of Ahstra's reaching hand. Pray it does not find us."

Syra inhaled Etháni's urgent warning, struggling to accept her words.

Halekar hurried them along, striding through the archway and into the gallery. The space was filled with stacks of metal containers, fifty centimetres in height and width. The ancient hammer insignia of the Národan was engraved upon each container.

Syra heard sturdy steps. As she glanced to her right, a malformed creature with a bulged forehead staggered from the corner of the gallery, reaching for Halekar. The beast growled and jutted its teeth at him.

The Kynorian ducked beneath its outstretched arms. He spun around, clamped its mouth shut and slammed his long blade into the base of its skull, preventing it from screeching. The beast convulsed as blood poured from its neck. Halekar silently dragged it to the floor and ripped the blade from its flesh. He wiped the blade before sheathing it.

To her shock, Syra noticed the hybrid monster wore pants and bore a bracelet and a gold ring. Its arms were more human-like than the scavenger rifas.

"Is it transforming?" Syra glanced at the wet, striped hair of the beast.

"Indeed, it is," Halekar whispered. "We must move."

A shudder swept through the underworld. They staggered in the after-tremors of the quake. The sound of crumbling stone trailed into the gallery, and the walls began to splinter, and then fracture. Debris drizzled from the separations in the ceiling.

The Kynorians locked eyes on the girls.

Screeches echoed beyond the gallery walls, causing Syra and Telora to recoil.

Etháni panned her light to the left, illuminating the T-section by the end of the gallery.

The snarling and grunting noises drew closer. Halekar and Etháni turned and sped Telora and Syra to the gallery's end.

Syra's leaden legs burned as she dashed vigorously.

Halekar slowed his pace, sheathed his sword, and aimed his light to the left of what appeared to be a T-section.

Syra could see a dark staircase elevating to the upper levels. "We must be close," she told Telora.

Reaching the first step of the staircase, Syra heard a cry from the opposite side of the T-section.

Etháni spun around and flashed her light into a two-by-three-metre room that looked more like a storage nook with rows of shelving on opposite walls. At the room's centre was a man chained to an X frame. His head was bowed, and his shredded shirt dangled below his waist Blood and saliva dripped down his nose and bearded chin. Upon his bicep was a festering bite mark.

"Help me," the man groaned, wriggling his shackles.

Syra crept forward, peering ahead. She knew his voice. Staring at the floor beneath his feet, she saw his scarf. Her voice quivered. "Tion . . . is that you?"

He outreached his shaky, blood-soaked hand, and she noticed all his fingers had been severed. He lifted his head, and she winced. His nose was purple and smeared. Brown welts covered his forehead as if he had been beaten with a hammer, and his eyes bled at their corners.

With a gasp, Syra stumbled. She felt nauseated at the deteriorated sight of him.

Tion tried to reach for her. "Syra, please help . . . me."

She rushed forward.

"Syra, no!" Halekar leaped after her.

As Syra entered the passage, Halekar grappled her by the waist, halting her before she crossed the door arch. He pinned her left foot to the floor with forceful pressure.

Ethári and Telora raced to Halekar's side.

"We have to save him," Syra insisted, pushing against Halekar's grip.

"Cease your movement, Syra," Ethári demanded, "and do not shift your left foot."

Syra froze and lowered her gaze.

She saw a thin wire bolted low on the left wall connected to a rod wedged into the corner of the opposite wall.

Halekar aimed his light at Syra's left foot. "Can you see it?" he asked her.

In her clear vision, she noticed the wire beneath her foot. Her heart smashed inside her ribcage.

CHAPTER 14
VOLATILE PREDATOR

As Halekar pressed against the bridge of her foot, a ferocious clamour of wrathful shrieks tore through the underworld. Snarls and growls rang above them. A metallic battering sound trailed along the cavities in the ceiling, and a jolting thump tremored the floor beneath their feet.

"Syra . . ." Tion called with a guttural voice, "they're coming for you. They'll kill you all." He vomited blood on the ground.

"We have to help him," Syra shouted at Halekar.

"Hold your pressure on the wire." His voice was swift. "Do not release it until I say."

He pressed his thumbs on opposite sides of her foot, pinning the wire to the floor.

Clicking and popping noises echoed through the passages, and a fierce roar sent the distant rifas into a frenzy.

"The rifas are coming!" Telora yelled.

Ethàni hauled Telora away and aimed her weapon light into the gallery. Ethàni's light caught the charging rifas.

"Slowly lift your foot off the wire," Halekar said.

Syra placed her weight on her rear leg. She inhaled a quick breath and removed her foot from the wire.

Halekar nodded. "Join the others."

"What about you?" Syra crept away from the doorway.

Hundreds of bestial rifas galloped along the passageway toward the gallery, barking and snarling.

"*Halekar, ese aronti!*" Ethání cried. They are coming.

She flung her last frost grenade through the archway of the gallery and fired. The frozen rifas shattered. The floor shook with the stomping footsteps of the giant rifa they had seen in the first chamber as it pummelled its way into the gallery.

Halekar sank to a deep squat as he held pressure on the wire. Glancing over his right shoulder, he screamed as he backflipped out of the doorway.

The pin popped. The wire twanged. A two-metre by three-metre spiked door came swinging through the passage with the force of a cyclone, whipping the air and slamming into the door arch. The thump of the barbed door tremored the gallery's foundations.

Syra flinched so hard she knocked into Telora.

The room fractured and crumbled. Tion screamed.

Syra stretched out her hand. "Tion!" she yelled.

With a booming crack, the passage caved in.

"To the staircase!" Ethání yelled, firing into the rifas flooding the gallery.

A grating scream erupted beyond the walls. The scavengers paused. Slapping steps hammered below them.

"The Aberrant," Halekar shouted. "We must reach the light. Stay behind me." He leaped into the staircase.

"Chase Halekar with all your strength." Ethání hauled Syra and Telora after him. "Do not look back."

Syra sprinted after him. Telora chased and climbed behind her. Vaulting the steps, Syra pumped her arms. Her legs burned, and her mouth dried as she sucked in the cold air.

Halekar spun through the landing and careered up the second staircase. The walls thumped. He shot his weapon as he reached the top of the stairs. The rifa corpse tumbled upon the steps, and the girls staggered as they leaped atop it to reach Halekar. He unsheathed his sword, gripping it in his left hand. Ethâni joined them, and she launched her last incendiary grenade into the stairs below.

They sprinted along a corridor with off-shooting paths. The explosion blazed yellow light into the corridor, trembling the floor and walls. Rifas came charging and screeching into the passage as the flames seared them. The Kynorians sliced and shot all in their path.

Syra dashed after Halekar as he crossed into a passage on the left. He lobbed the head off a rifa and pulverised another with his Isoburst. At the end of the passage, he swivelled and sprinted onto the main corridor.

Syra felt her lungs surging. She glanced over her shoulder.

Rifas leaped upon Ethâni, and her axe zinged as she severed their limbs. Her orange plasma ignited the corridor.

Halekar jumped upon a row of tables, evading the clawing, raging monsters filling the room.

Syra and Telora leaped after him with Ethâni at the rear.

Telora yelped. Syra gasped at her failing voice.

A scavenger rifa dragged Telora to the floor. Syra swung and buried her axe into the beast's skull.

The warrioress nodded at Syra as she gathered Telora from the floor and sped them along the passage.

They entered a broad, empty hall as the rifas relentlessly chased them like a horde of voracious savages. Syra saw dual entry doors at the end of the hall. The terror of the beasts' snarls rumbled metres away.

With only thirty metres to reach the doors, she could feel her leaden legs stumbling beneath her.

Halekar burst through the doors. One by one, they dove inside. He slammed the doors shut and collected a recurved iron rod lying atop a nearby table. He jammed the rod through the handles, barring it.

The room was filled with metal containers. Inside them were thin, metallic scrolls etched with glyphs and symbols. The Kynorians and the girls marched to a locked door at the end of the room.

Syra hunched, placing her hands on her knees as she struggled to catch her breath. She glanced up at Telora.

Telora was clasping the back of her head. Her face was pale, and she stumbled as she steadied herself against a nearby table.

Syra lifted her. "You're bleeding," she said, inspecting her sister's blood-soaked hand.

The double doors shook as the monsters crashed against them.

Etháni spun Telora and shone her light on her wound. She stared at Halekar. "*Esi dánkoma.*"

Halekar stared into Etháni's eyes. "*Dánkoma?*" His eyes widened.

"I feel sick." Telora clutched her chest.

"What are you saying, Etháni?" Syra asked, "and what's happening to my sister?"

The Kynorians gave no response. Halekar sheathed his sword and slung his Isoburst onto his shoulder. He aimed his light at Telora's head while Etháni removed a vial with a bright yellow liquid inside from her cloak.

"Your sister has been bitten by a scavenger," Etháni said bluntly. "This serum will suppress the pathogen, but she does not have long." She lifted the vial to Telora's lips. "Sip a mouthful."

Syra's heart sank. "Have long for what?" she questioned, staring at her faint sister.

Etháni poured the rest of the liquid onto Telora's head before peering into Halekar's eyes.

He removed what appeared to be a reticulated glass strap from inside his cloak. The transparent bracelet pulsed with blue light.

He clasped Telora's arm. "This might hurt when it attaches to your skin." He stared into her eyes.

"What's it going to do to her?" Syra asked.

"Keep the poison inside her contained," Halekar said. "The scavenger strain was designed to transform mortals into rifas and after years of pain, savagery, and suffering, inevitably kill them."

The room fell to silence as the rifas dispersed beyond the double doors. Their pounding footsteps trailed away from their position.

Syra's mouth hung agape at his finite words. Gazing into Telora's bloodshot eyes, she felt her strength falter. *I've finally found you, and now this.* Her voice wavered. "Can she be healed?"

The Kynorians locked their gaze. Silence removed any remaining hope Syra desperately clutched onto. She could hear her rising blood pressure throbbing beneath her temples.

"We must bring Telora to Starfall," Halekar said.

"Will she die?" Syra asked with a choked voice.

Ethâni placed her warm hand on Syra's shoulder. "We must hope she can be saved."

"What if we're attacked again?" Syra protested.

Halekar pierced her with his glare. "The axe you carry is no mortal weapon. An artefact from a previous age, the axe was designed to slay rifas." Halekar removed a seven-inch transparent rail from his vest and aimed it at the axe.

He clasped Syra's forehead, and a thin stream of shimmering blue light beamed from the device to the axe.

Syra stared at the axe, and she felt a current of electricity inject into her fingers, spreading into her hand and forearm. Images of Kynorian warriors wielding the axe were transmitted into her mind. Syra closed her eyes and began to breathe long, slow breaths.

A calmness permeated her mind, and in her mild reverie, a combat knowledge from the ancient past transferred to her as if accessing it for the first time.

The beam of light between Halekar's rail severed, and with a slight vibration from the axe handle, the images vanished. He removed his hand from her forehead and slid the device inside his vest.

Syra opened her eyes and gazed upon the axe.

Halekar faced Telora and fed the bracelet onto her hand. "You should feel a momentary pinch." He waved his hand across its glowing blue light.

A bright red light flashed from the bracelet, and it chimed and beeped. Telora clasped her arm and screamed with such high amplitude her voice cracked, and she fell to the floor. Syra gripped her hand, lifted her, and steadied her on her feet.

The room's ceiling shook with tremendous force. Stomping feet hammered the floor. Surrounding screeches and shrieks reverberated about them.

"The bio-marker of the bracelet," Etháni said. "It has drawn the attention of the Aberrant."

"The vile creature comes for her." Halekar power-lifted Telora, straddling her upon his left shoulder. Holding his Isoburst, he shot the lock on the door at the rear of the room. With a stabbing thrust, he kicked the door wide open.

CHAPTER 15
FORCES OF LIGHT

ETHÁNI DRAGGED the dazed Syra into action as the rifas breached the barred door. Etháni and Syra sped across the door arch and chased Halekar along a narrow bridge. They climbed a set of steps to the machine room, filled with metal struts and pipes. Scavengers charged at Halekar from both sides.

Halekar sidestepped and fired, killing three beasts.

Syra glanced over her shoulder and saw a rifa swipe at Etháni. The warrioress clamped its arm and launched it over her shoulder, slamming the creature upon the floor. She leaped ahead like a panthera, pushing Syra forward.

Halekar dashed along a short passage that led to a long room, and he leaped upon a large pipe.

Syra jumped after him and gasped at the ten-metre drop beneath her, filled with shrieking rifas. "So many of them. Where are they coming from."

"Head up," Etháni urged her. "Keep moving."

Syra balanced herself as she ran along the pipe.

Ahead, Halekar vaulted onto a parallel beam leading to

an opening. He fired his weapon at the monsters filling the passage winding to the right.

Syra felt her axe vibrating and flashing red. A rifa squawked and jumped in front of her. She lifted the axe and swung, slicing a wedge in the beast's neck. She screamed and dashed after Halekar.

Syra saw Telora reaching her hand out to her. "Hold on, Telora," she cried. "Hold on."

"*Ese montar, Halekar,*" Etháni yelled from behind, firing at the monsters. *It is drawing near.*

The jugular growl of the Aberrant swept into the passage behind them. Syra heard its rasping breaths as she pursued Halekar onto a wooden ramp leading to a vast hall. The chasing rifas snarled, snapped, and barked.

Syra glimpsed natural light streaming through pillars high upon the hall's walls.

Halekar shouted back at them. "We must reach the light! The exit is here." He pointed ahead.

In her blurred vision, Syra saw a double door at the end of the grand hallway. Thin slithers of light emanated from the door frame like a fire-lit beacon of a heavenly sanctuary.

Hundreds of scavengers filled the hall, and hybrids scaled the lower balconies above them. Halekar slaughtered the first wave of rifas.

"Halekar, to your right," Syra yelled.

A hybrid barged through a pack of scavengers and slammed into Halekar, grappling his waist. His Isoburst slipped from his grasp on impact, sliding across the floor.

Etháni switched to rapid-fire mode and destroyed the second wave of hybrids charging toward Halekar. The monsters wailed to their deaths.

The Kynorian prince fastened Telora against his shoulder. He clamped the hybrid's arm. Stepping across its legs, he twisted his hip and slammed it onto the floor. The beast thrashed and clawed. He unsheathed his blade and thrust the tip into its neck.

Rifas scuttled past Halekar, charging at Syra. She screamed as she chopped at the first rifa, sending it tumbling to the floor. She cleaved the chest of the next beast and heard the sizzling singe of the axe blade cauterising its flesh.

Halekar leaped to his feet and collected his Isoburst. He spun and fired at the rifas barricading the exit.

The Aberrant stormed into the corridor, leaping like an enraged reptilian. The superbeast ploughed its way to Etháni, roaring with its kinetic jaw opened.

"Halekar!" Etháni screamed.

A sudden flux of screeches advanced from the side paths. Hundreds of rifas poured into the hall.

Sweat streamed down Syra's face. Her arms thrashed. She could not breathe fast enough. She withdrew her father's blade from its sheath at the sight of the massing rifa horde.

Etháni threw her last shock grenade into a pack of scavengers tearing and screeching behind her. Electricity strikes cauterised the rifas, and they convulsed and squealed on the floor.

Halekar, Syra, and Etháni sprinted. Twenty metres away to reach the exit. Bursts of plasma fired. Ten metres away. Five metres.

Syra cried in the ecstasy of seeing the sunlight glinting through the doors' edges.

Like a teleporting shadow, Halekar rushed forward and burst through the doors. The blinding sunlight beamed in Syra's eyes as she crossed the threshold. Etháni vaulted through the archway, swinging her axe at a scavenger's neck.

A rifa charged, lunging upon Syra in the open air. Its skin sizzled and smoked in the sunlight. It seized her neck and thrust its teeth at her throat. She drove her father's blade into its neck and flung its corpse to the side.

Five more rifas charged at them in attack, but they fell to the ground, shrieking and sizzling in the sun.

Ethàni lifted Syra to her feet. Halekar stood like a Kynorian king, with the limp body of Telora across his shoulder.

The rifas crowded the doorway, snarling and barking. Ghoulish beasts serving the darkness dared not step into the light.

A deep growl caused the rifas to skulk from the exit as the Aberrant stomped across the threshold and into the sunlight. Its skin hissed and smoked in the light, but the superbeast raised its clawed hand and pointed to Halekar. Thrusting its face forward, it unleashed a bellowing roar. Bloody saliva sprayed from its opened mouth. Its eyes flashed yellow and red before returning to white.

Syra gasped at the immense size of the Aberrant, and she stepped behind Ethàni.

"Go back to your pit!" Ethàni yelled.

Halekar pointed to the sun. "Or burn in the light!"

The superbeast held its fierce gaze. With a searing screech, it leaped backward and out of the sun's rays. Its hunched shoulders rose and fell as it inhaled and exhaled rasping breaths. With a final growl, it wrenched its body and disappeared into the blackness of the Dura Mines.

The scavengers inched forward into the archway snarling and screeching. The hybrids pounded their fists upon the doors taunting the Kynorians in their dark mode of tongue.

"We must not tarry here," Halekar urged.

Syra faced Halekar. "Will they come after us?"

"The rifas will gather by nightfall," Halekar said, shielding his eyes from the setting sun. "The Aberrant will track your sister."

Syra sheathed her blade and her axe and caressed Telora's hand. "She's burning up."

Etháni lifted Telora's head and dripped a few drops of the *viata* elixir into her mouth. "This shall aid in regulating her temperature."

"Come now," Halekar urged, "let us find safer places to converse. We must reach the coast of the Sistilus Gulf before nightfall. May our feet be swift, for these Aberrants sense all during the night."

Syra felt the fading sun warming her cold, numb face. She might have felt comforted if not for the snarling voices of the baleful rifas hissing from the opening.

Halekar avoided the ancient bluestone thoroughfare leading northbound. Instead, he guided them along a descending track snaking through a sparse forest of larn trees. Following the shores of the running creek, he guided them westward and up toward the slopes of the rocky foothills drawing closer to the shoreline.

Syra heard birds chirping and the flutter of their wings as they landed from branch to branch. Her fear of the rifas slowly slipped away, and her pace eased to a steady march. She inhaled the cool and refreshing air as it streamed across the native grasses beside the track.

After ascending a steep pathway, the ground levelled, and the trees receded. Before her eyes, she saw the coastline of the Sistilus Gulf in the distance. The sun had set beyond the treetops of the Promiseus forest, veiling the lands in a dark auburn shimmer.

After striding four kilometres from the edges of the woodland, Halekar descended stone steps, which lowered onto an old port with a short pier. Syra inhaled the salty sea mists as she marched along. Tethered to the pillars of the dock drifted a dark grey ship forty feet in length. He climbed aboard and waited for Syra and Etháni to board.

Descending the steps, Syra could see a desolate barn and two small outhouses at the end of a winding path. The barn doors had been removed, and the rear wall of the first outhouse lay in ruin upon the ground. A heap of broken chairs littered the entrance of the barn.

"I came here three summers back," Syra told Etháni, "and there were people everywhere. This place is dead." She crossed onto the pier and boarded the ship.

Etháni turned and gazed upon the stone path from which they had come. "Many of Númaria's shores are no longer safe. "She untethered the rope from the cleat of the pier and leaped onboard.

Inside the hull, Halekar motioned to Syra. "Please sit down. Telora shall need your presence."

She sat on the soft leatherbound bench beneath the ship's canopy, and Halekar gently lowered Telora beside her.

Syra cradled Telora in her lap. She had never understood her enduring love for her sister until that critical point in time. A moment of uncertainty. A moment of life and death.

Telora's eyes slowly opened. "Don't be upset; you found me," she said with a slurred voice. "We'll be safe with them. They'll take care of us."

Syra felt a warmth in her heart. "I was always going to find you, even if it killed me."

Telora closed her eyes, and her body sank into Syra's arms as if she had been sleeping for hours.

Etháni placed her palm on Telora's forehead. "Her fever has eased." Etháni closed her eyes as if she was accessing a higher sense of awareness. "She walks upon the fringes of the firmament. Her heart lingers in the comfort of joining the kindred spirits of the Hydroverse."

A tear welled in Syra's eye, but she wiped the droplet in shame. "I don't want her to leave me. I just found her. I love her too much."

"Indeed," Halekar said, "you demonstrated love in action by endangering your life to find her. Navigating the infested paths of the Dura Mines is no small feat one should place aside. Verily, you must find truth and solace in such a valorous act."

Syra gazed upon Halekar's face. "What if she doesn't wake up, or worse, what if she turns into one of those monsters from the mines?"

Halekar peered into Ethâni's eyes before facing Syra. "A scavenger bite yields our deep concern." He stared upon the swaying waves of the gulf. "All one can do in such days is be prepared for the unknown. These are times of war, and our enemy's hands have been fervently at work."

"With each new time cycle of the enemy," Ethâni said, "came evolved forms of monsters. At first, the bipedal rifas ravaged settlements across the western lands. The human-like hybrids emerged from the Mountains of Atanimax in the north, wielding weapons and the language of our enemy known as the *Dark Mode*. The bestial quadruped rifas with furs and fangs sprang from the underworld, designed as bio-weapons to depopulate Númaria." She paused and focused her steely gaze upon Syra. "With the arrival of these Aberrants, one can only imagine the perils of the coming days, months, and years."

Syra brushed the fringe of Telora's hair and feared the days of tribulation ahead. In her anxiety, she considered the plausible outcomes of her situation. She pondered hope and all its intangible falsehoods and contemplated her survival amid the likelihood of death.

Etháni inched closer to Syra. "Telora's future is uncertain. In Starfall, all shall be done in her aid."

"Our world has changed," Syra said. "I can feel it and see it all around Netidum and Lakomea. We have formed a local militia called the Firekites to fight against tyranny, but the Denkarians are too powerful. Each uprising is quelled with extreme force."

Halekar powered the marine vessel and steered it toward the fading sun. "Pass the letter you hold to the leader of the Firekites," he told Syra. "Their aid will be necessary to infiltrate the perverse political systems of your people. At the very least cause a distraction against Ahstra's viceroys."

"Ahstra has returned to Númaria," Etháni told her. "An ancient evil thought gone; he has set in motion such dire events one cannot fathom. With his nefarious reign, depraved acts and countless horrors shall become more frequent within the lands of the mortals. The Denkarian officials and elites are corrupted, serving Ahstra's will now."

"Who is Ahstra?" Syra asked. "You mentioned that name earlier in the mines."

"Ahstra is the destroyer of civilisations," Halekar replied, "a foul spirit indentured to decimate Númaria's population and enslave the few remaining. Our collective errand is one of great urgency. Etháni and I have been mandated to survey the northwestern lands to aid two compelling individuals similar in age to you, Syra."

Syra scoffed. "They're my age, and they're compelling? Who are these 'individuals' you speak of?"

Etháni's laden eyes beamed, and facing Syra, she lowered her voice to a whisper. "Within them rests the fate of every soul on Númaria. Guided by Santia, a powerful leader, their great mission must be achieved."

Syra lifted her gaze to Halekar. "Inside the mines, you did something to me. How can I wield an axe without any prior knowledge? It's as if I magically knew how to fight, but I've never been trained to fight."

"I am not solely responsible," Halekar told her. "I merely guided you toward possibility. A young woman of assured courage, you inevitably connected with the knowledge of the weapon through the Hydroverse." He gave her a soft smile. "This awakening phenomenon is known to the Kynorians as an alignment to *right action, in the moment.*"

Syra's forehead creased. "Hydroverse."

Halekar nodded. "A force, an ethereal urge that controls all awareness and life. The Hydroverse, our ancestors believed, became manifest by the one infinite entity that reigns supreme. A cosmological creator."

Syra stared at the heavens, past the stringy clouds above the fringes of the horizon.

Stars glinted in the darkening skies as if to communicate with her, and a sense of wonder filled her heart.

"Your courage has proven promising, mortal," Etháni said. "I ordain you a defender of the truth. You are an *Ark of Light* amid the darkness." She waved her hand above Syra's head, and the jewel on Etháni's ring glowed like the white and blue lights of the Hydroverse.

Syra felt a smooth vibration through her chest and shoulders. A warm luminance caressed her face.

"Your training shall begin in Starfall," Etháni said. "In the coming days, you shall learn such truths that would strain the hearts of your kindred. In time, you may need to unlearn mistruths about your existence. Though such revelations are confronting, you must be willing to embrace them. We shall guide you and prepare you for the coming war."

Syra felt a spectral gloom overshadow her mind. *War*, she pondered, not ever knowing its total reach, but she had seen death enough times. After a stream of doubtful thoughts, she felt her spirits lighten.

She inhaled a deep breath and slowly released it. *I'm an Ark of Light . . .* The westerly winds streamed through her hair as the ship cruised upon the rocking waves.

Syra stared into Etháni's eyes. "I guess I'm caught up in all of this now."

HORDE OF THE
UNDERWORLD

Thank you for reading **Horde of the Underworld!**

I would love to hear your opinion of this book in a review on your favourite book retailer's site.

The Journey Continues
Discover the struggles of planet Númaria in my premier book series, **The War for Ascension**. Unveil new secrets and adventures by reading the following volumes in the *Ascension Archive.*

Register for my mailing list, and you'll become a WFA 'Inner Circle' member where you'll receive a secret stash of free goodies! You'll also gain access to all upcoming book and music releases.

Register Here:
WWW.DOMINICIANGENNARI.COM

ACKNOWLEDGMENTS

Edited by Diann T. Read

Thank you to my *Freedom Fighting* family, Scotty Saks, Sacha Stone, Joanne Aarstol, Hayley Jackson, Carly and Julia (Soul Twins), and Maria Crisler.

A very special measure of gratitude must be given to Kyle Kemper for his guidance and support, and may we continue to create the decentralised free world we desire.

My eternal love goes to Rubina and Atreyu.

My thanks go to the fantasy genius Matt Wright for being a foundational pillar during the creation of this story.

To all the brave men and women who enacted courage and deep wisdom during these times of extremes, I salute you. To my loyal supporters who continue to stand by my side, may all our dreams of a better world manifest into reality.

ABOUT THE AUTHOR

Dominician Gennari is an author, a researcher, and a freedom fighter. Having turned down Hollywood and millions of dollars, Dominician is focused on writing wholesome mythological stories that inspire  and awaken humanity. As a mentee of the late David Farland and a member of Apex Writers, he further developed his skills to carve out his epic tale **The War for Ascension**. Dominician is also a recording artist and frontman of the *Epic-Industrial-Metal* band **Ark of Light**.

He currently lives in Melbourne, Australia.

Visit The Official Websites:

WWW.DOMINICIANGENNARI.COM
WWW.ARKOFLIGHT.NET

www.ingramcontent.com/pod-product-compliance
Lightning Source LLC
Chambersburg PA
CBHW030412120726
47904CB00007B/2251